Nura
and the
Immortal Palace

"With gorgeous, atmospheric writing, M.T. Khan tells a
bold tale that challenges greed and inequality as the
tough and clever Nura fights the odds from the mica
mines of rural Pakistan to a realm of jinn and magic."
Xiran Jay Zhao

"Sparkling with magic… A twisty, atmospheric tale with
a fierce protagonist, whose voice lingered in my mind
long after I'd finished reading."
Jennifer Bell

"It was a delight to adventure with Nura into the
magical and luminous world of the jinn."
Jasbinder Bilan

"Both startling and beautiful. Nura will win your heart
in the first pages of this magical adventure
with surprises at every turn."
J.C. Cervantes

Amir
and the
Jinn Princess

M.T. KHAN

WALKER
BOOKS

First published 2024 by Walker Books Ltd
87 Vauxhall Walk, London SE11 5HJ

2 4 6 8 10 9 7 5 3 1

Text © 2024 Maeeda Khan
Cover and interior illustrations © 2024 Hazem Asif

The right of Maeeda Khan to be identified as author of this work has been asserted in accordance with the Copyright, Designs and Patents Act 1988

This book has been typeset in ITC Berkeley Oldstyle Std

Printed and bound in Great Britain by CPI Group (UK) Ltd

British Library Cataloguing in Publication Data: a catalogue record for this book is available from the British Library

ISBN 978-1-5295-0920-5

www.walker.co.uk

MIX
Paper | Supporting
responsible forestry
FSC® C171272

To my sisters
for being my first friends

Prologue

It was an endless field of bricks and clay, of smoke and fire, and words and sway.

I was just a baby then, a bundle of giggles and round eyes, clinging on to Baba as he strolled over the world, *his* world, and spoke to me like I'd own it all one day. That the smoke curling out of the chimneys drew circles in the sky for me. That each man toiling under the sun did so because they served me. That every brick with Baba's name on it was also mine, because we shared our last name, our family legacy, our reputation and all the riches that came with it.

"This could be yours."

He spread his arms like an eagle, summoning the sun to wash over the kiln in glorious golden rays. I couldn't deny it. Watching it all from above, every move, the mechanical efficiency, our name on each brick in the towering piles – even then, I knew it was grand.

"*You see, the reason we stand up here and those men below us, is because our family has worked hard for generations. We're smarter than others. Stronger. Sharper. That's why we sit at the top, Amir.*"

I stuck a finger in my mouth, babbling around it. "*Why they no smart?*"

"*It's in their nature. Their fathers were lazy and dull, and spent all their money on cigarettes. A person's wealth is decided by their decisions. When you look at someone poor, know that they made the wrong ones.*"

"*Bad decision,*" I repeated, not knowing what the words even meant.

"*Yes, beta, bad decisions.*"

I didn't know it then, but I know it now. Just how much a string of choices can change the course of destiny, the status of a name, and the impression of a face.

And how decisions may not be decisions at all.

CHAPTER 1

On Top of the World

"Do you know why you're here, Mr Rafiq?"

"Here" is the inside of the headmistress's office, her desk square and imposing, shelves lined neatly with thick books, and the floor tiles clean – too clean, glaringly spotless, as if she'd scrubbed away the evidence of a crime. The smile she sends my way is forced, running out of patience as my attention skips round everything but her question. How much longer can I make her wait? I've been in this seat before. It's all too familiar. She'll start wringing her hands, smile fading, and then lean back in her leather chair with a shake of her head.

Headmistress Baqil performs the moves as if I've given her stage directions. Here comes her sigh right now. "Amir, you're some—"

"Someone we care deeply about. You were an ace student. I know you've gone through a tough time, but this behaviour is not what we expect from you," I finish for her, reciting the speech she's given time and time again. It's often followed by: *You used to get amazing grades. It's still possible, Amir. Why don't you just try?*

There's no point.

Headmistress Baqil swallows, clearing her throat. She shifts her attention to the two boys on either side of me, one with a bruised lip and the other with a black eye. Unlike them, my own face is flawless, which makes me the centre of suspicion. It may look like I've given them the beating of a lifetime, but look at my knuckles – there's not a single scratch on them.

"You two. You said Amir is the reason you fought. That Amir set you up to blame each other. How is that possible?"

The one to my left, whose name I don't even remember, sputters forward. "All I wanted was to be Amir's friend! But he told me I had to become the class representative. That's why I tried to steal the job from Abdul."

Abdul grunts, chair screeching as he leans in too. "That's not all. Amir said I could be his friend if I won the next track race. But everyone knows Mustafa is the fastest runner... I stole his running shoes so he wouldn't be able to participate."

"So what I'm hearing," I interject, "is that you two fought over me? How sweet."

"Amir," the headmistress scolds. I shrug. She rubs her temples and releases a long breath. "Why would you ask them to do that?"

The truth is, I never expected them to do it. I have boys coming up to me every day wanting to hold my books or tag along after class. Leeches, all of them. This may be a wealthy private school filled with the sons of aristocrats, businessmen and politicians, but I'm still quite high on the food chain. I'm Amir Rafiq, youngest of three potential heirs to one of Pakistan's largest brick companies. I get driven everywhere I go, eat lobster with truffle oil for dinner, and there's no inch of me that isn't covered in designer brands. According to the hierarchy of life, I'm better than everyone else. Don't mistake that as my opinion. It's just facts.

These two are prime examples of why. Mustafa's baba owns a distribution company, and I'm sure his family just wants a partnership with mine to ship our bricks around Pakistan. Abdul, on the other hand, has a sister approaching her mid-twenties, which means every second she's not married is another stain on their family name. My cousin is her perfect match – or at least that's what Abdul's mother thinks. I'm not sure they even know each other's names.

That's why it's useless making friends when you're me. When someone looks my way, they don't just see me, they see what's *around* me: wealth, a network of connections, and a future enjoying a top-paying job at my father's company with a lifestyle most people couldn't dream of. Every handshake is a business deal, and each friendly smile is an alliance pact. Anything important is passed down to me through my baba, and from his baba before him – connections, money, and a purpose in life.

I know exactly where I stand. And it's not at the start of a path that I have any role in choosing.

But the headmistress doesn't want the truth. The truth doesn't work in situations like this. What does is simple: a flash of power.

"Are you really blaming *me*, Headmistress Baqil?" I cross my legs. "My family has donated to this school for generations. We even started a scholarship for less fortunate students. I would never want to create a ruckus at this fine establishment. All I hoped was that Mustafa and Abdul would strive to be better in their academics and sports. Is that horrible of me to ask?"

The headmistress's cheeks flush like she's been slapped. She coughs out her next sentence. "Of course not, Amir. It's rather nice of you to look out for your classmates like that."

My lips curl into a smile. "Thank you."

"This isn't fair, Headmistress – I didn't mean to hit Abdul. It must've been a jinn that possessed me!"

"Y–yeah, someone must've put nazar on me. I wouldn't ever do this normally."

Leave it to these two morons to blame jinn, curses, kala jadu, and not their own greed. Just last week I saw Abdul punch our resident nerd for the answers to Wednesday's test. But it *must* be nazar. Totally.

I thought only uneducated people believed that superstitious nonsense.

Nazar is the evil eye, when jealous people put curses on you to bring about your ruin. And kala jadu, or black magic, is that hodgepodge of destructive spells and jinxes. And don't get me started on jinn. Invisible beings of fire and smoke? Tricksters who take advantage of you when your guard's down? They're nothing more than bedtime tales my cousins and I share to get a fright out of one another. So many troubled people will blame kala jadu or jinn for their downfall. But how about looking in a mirror and realizing it's just you and your filthy luck? I know. It's hard. I've done it, and I haven't seen the world the same since.

The headmistress smacks the desk with a heavy hand. "Save it. Mustafa, Abdul, I'll be calling your families tonight. We do not tolerate violence here at Lahore Boys Grammar School. If this happens again, suspension will be on the table."

Abdul and Mustafa launch out of their seats to object, but one glance at my relaxed posture and they fold back into themselves, heads low as they nod.

"This won't happen again," they say in unison.

The bell rings just as this dry conversation finishes. I'm up, slinging my bag over my shoulder and waving without turning back. Down the halls, classes are noisy with the restlessness of the end of the day, and the end of school. It's the last day before summer holidays. In ten minutes, my driver will be here, and I won't have to see any of these whiny brats for another two months.

Usually, I'd stick around for an hour or two, flicking through the reading list for next term, but that was the old Amir. The new me knows it's not going to make a difference. I'm a Rafiq. Born into a family that made the right decisions long ago so I wouldn't have to make my own now. If I'm cruising along a river leading to success, there's no reason I should try to swim against its current.

"Hey." A meaty hand lands on my shoulder, spinning me around. I'm face-to-face with Abdul's ugly mug, his black eye staring me down. "We're getting in trouble because of *you*."

"Me?" I ask, fake shock strumming through my voice. "Weren't you the one who got caught stealing Mustafa's shoes? And you, Mustafa, you couldn't have been more obvious about hijacking the votes for class representative. You both sicken me."

"Us?" Mustafa scoffs in disbelief. "You're the one who cut off all your friendships last year. Ever since your mama ran away you've become such a—"

I stomp towards them, fists clenched.

Relax, Amir. Deep breath in. Deep breath out. *They're not worth it.*

"Keep my name and everything to do with me out of your mouths," I snap. "Or that suspension might come sooner than you think."

My nails dig into the straps of my bag. Without sparing them another glance, I march through the door.

Within the manicured school gardens, the afternoon sun is harsh. My skin feels like it's burning. Like I'm being boiled from the inside out. I'd gone without thinking of Mama the entire day. Why does the collar of my uniform feel so much tighter now? I'm suffocating. I can't breathe—

"*Meow.*"

A ball of fur brushes against my leg. Red eyes and a coat of black fur – it's one of those devil spawns. A cat.

My servants spend at least a good hour cleaning my uniform and ironing it every day. Now this cat's just gone and mussed up my trousers with its fur. I nudge it away, but it meows again, nuzzling its head against my ankle.

Another five minutes and my driver should be here. In another five minutes this clingy cat won't be my problem. But until then, even my heart, despite its dark core, can spare a crumb or two. I reach into my pocket and pull out a pack of gachak. Crouching next to the cat, I notice its coat almost reflects a dark blue in the sunlight. I dump the gachak biscuits in front of the cat. It stares at me with glittering crimson orbs like it's asking whether I'm offering poison, but when I shrug, it moves forward, crunching down on the biscuits.

I'm not feeding it because I like cats. Nor am I feeding it because Mama used to do the same thing to the strays that weaselled their way into our garden. I'm doing it to get rid of those stale biscuits. It's not like I was planning to eat them in the first place.

The cat finishes them with a hunger I didn't realize it possessed. But the cat thinks I'm a good person, because next thing I know it's nuzzling against my leg again, purring. I guess I could offer a little pat. My fingers rest on its fuzzy head, soft and silky. The cat meows, scrunching its eyes as if smiling at me.

"Amir!"

A hand waves to me from the car park. My driver is here, standing outside the sleek black Mercedes that's one of my baba's favourites. I take a step towards it, but my leg stops before I can swing it forward. That pesky cat – it's tugging on my trousers.

"Quit it." I try to shake it off. "I already gave you food."

But here's the thing about those devil spawns: they know the art of enchantment. Red orbs growing bigger by the second, head bowed, and tail tucked politely, it's hypnotizing me without even uttering a meow.

"Greedy leech." I surrender. Shuffling things around in my bag, I make enough room for the cat and plop it inside. It purrs as it makes itself comfy. I throw the flap over just so my driver doesn't start asking questions. As long as this cat keeps quiet, I guess I could snatch it up something heartier for dinner. It does look rather skinny.

"Sit tight," I demand.

We settle into the back of the car, leather seats soothing. In the brief moment that I shut my eyes, everything disappears: the exhaustion of waking at the crack of dawn; trudging through classes that can't hold my attention; the mundane feeling of walking through a life already figured out for me. In this moment, with the window down and wind blowing in my face, I can pretend I'm not Amir Rafiq, the twelve-year-old youngest son of one of Pakistan's richest businessmen, sitting at the top of the world. I'm air. I'm weightless. I'm just a kid with a cat in his backpack.

I'm not the culmination of a century of decisions I can't afford to change.

CHAPTER 2

An Endless Ladder

The dinner table is a painting. Bright, colourful biryani marks the centre, while platters of kebabs, koftas and salads blossom outward. The raita adds a nice pop of white against blazing red tandoori chicken. Glistening naans and rotis frame the corners, and tall glasses of lassi shimmer under the chandelier, still cold enough to collect dew on the surface. After a long, tedious day, I could devour it all.

"Amir." An old lady stretches out her arms, caging me in a hug. Her bristly, ironed hair pokes my forehead. "There's my grandson."

"Assalaamu alaikum," I greet her, voice strained. If she squeezes any harder, my ribcage might collapse.

Tonight's dinner is supposed to be an important one, or so Dadi said. She has an announcement to make. Good news or bad, when it comes from Dadi,

I just know it's going to be a thorn poking at my side.

We pull into our seats at the long dinner table. Servants are still bringing over dishes. One has a jug of lassi in his hand, waiting to top up any glasses if need be. Another makes sure each plate catches the light perfectly. The last one flits about the dining room, checking everything is in order: the Quranic wood calligraphy, the display of Multani pottery, some fancy crystal lamps my baba bought in Turkey, and the spotless mosaic flooring.

Just like the cat I hid inside my room, I've worked up an appetite. Which dish would it like best? Maybe I can scrape some flakes off the barramundi. Cats like fish, don't they?

"Your dada's on a business trip, so he'll be missing dinner with us." Dadi ruffles my hair. "Don't worry, I'm sure he'll bring you many gifts."

I suppress a groan. But I am no more miserable than usual. My grandfather's presence at the estate means everyone walks on eggshells, Baba included. Dada's got the temper of a sailor and keeps forgetting that he's brought me the same gift from his last four business trips: a gold-plated Quran. *"Better read up, beta. Every prayer you do is another good deed added to me. Aha-ha!"* I wonder why he can't just make his own prayers. Too busy, he'd probably explain.

Even with servants fluttering about and Dadi's arms wrapped around my core, the estate feels empty. Dry. Dead. Each servant is a robot computing their tasks, whizzing from one corner to the other with vacant, numb expressions.

It wasn't always like this.

When Mama was around, I awoke to the sound of sitar strums, her chiming voice drifting across the estate like a call to prayer. She began and ended each day the same – playing music. She could enchant anything: instruments or people. I'd often find her in the kitchen, fingers scooping up some of the chef's chutneys and humming in gratitude. Or in the courtyard, asking the gardener how the flowers grow so bright. Servants would chatter like a flock of morning birds in her presence. She had a way of welcoming people, of making them feel special, no matter if they were an important investor or lowly kitchen sweeper.

And whenever I came home from school, Mama would be waiting there for me in the study, ready to throw away my textbooks and show me a new novel she'd uncovered in our century-old library.

A heavy smack on my shoulder startles me out of my thoughts. It means that Ashar, my older brother, has graced us with his presence today.

"How was school?" Ashar asks me, gaze landing straight on the chaat.

"Boring."

"What about the tutor? He said your grades have been dropping."

"It's nothing the next test can't fix." Truly, no one cares if I fail or plunge below the average. With the right connections and sneaky manoeuvres, my future maintains its brightness. I'm not the one in control anyway.

"What will I do with such a genius brother? What if you outshine me?" Ashar chuckles, but his voice lacks any warmth. When I don't respond, he backtracks to keep me peaceful. "But that's impossible. You don't have my sunny smile."

He smiles widely to show his point, and it's true, I have to squint to prevent myself from burning at its intensity. It's the smile he uses for everything – favours, extra cash and luring people to his side.

"Amir's only got eyes for horse riding." The chair next to me shuffles, and my fifteen-year-old sister, Alishba, takes a seat. "Didn't you finish the hardest course yesterday? I heard you're good enough to join the youth league."

News travels faster than I thought. Or rather, my siblings know exactly what we're all doing and when.

"The instructor is just flattering me. Plenty of us are good enough for the league."

"But you're also great at cards, playing the rabab, reading quickly – and remember that one time you tried your hand at chess? You learned it in ten minutes and beat the neighbour's uncle."

Despite the praise, Alishba's voice is rigid, as if she's pressing me to make some kind of confession. When she asks her next question, I understand the reason. "Why don't you actually hone any of those skills? Who knows, you might prefer it to Baba's boring old brick company."

There it is. Those little sneaky manoeuvres. It's like holding someone's hand only to lead them into a burning forest. Alishba doesn't want me in the running for heir of Baba's company. As the middle child, she already has a much bigger threat – our older brother. But nothing misses her radar. No matter how indifferent I am, she still sees me as a rival.

"There'd be no point," I counter. Think about it. Why would I bother with petty skills or competitive horse riding if I know where my future lies? I don't need any of that to be an executive at Baba's company. Whether I enjoy them or not doesn't matter. Passion, purpose … they're just distractions against an end we all know I can't escape.

"What is all this talk about rabab and chess and my boring old brick company?"

The table snaps into attention as Baba makes his way to the head seat, settling down on the plush cushion. His hands are folded, eyes creased, and a streak of grey hair shoots down his scalp. He looks at us expectantly.

"Assalaamu alaikum," we all greet in unison. Now that he's finally lifted his fork and taken the first bite of kebab, we're free to dig in.

Ashar goes for the chaat, while Alishba scoops up biryani and I grab a samosa. I could fill my entire stomach with just these.

"Did the meeting go well?" Dadi pipes up, barely half a roti on her plate. She's more interested in analysing Baba's expression, hawk eyes determined.

"Never been better," he replies not a beat later. "The reserves are still full. And production's only been getting more efficient."

Dadi hums and returns to her plate, satisfied for now.

Alishba eats one spoonful before breaking into her daily report. "I read that bricks are very energy efficient. They absorb sunlight throughout the day, and then release that energy at night."

"Correct." Baba nods.

"And…" Alishba trails off, her leg shaking under the table, "the minerals inside the bricks are what determine the colour of it!"

Some *boring* brick company now. Alishba's practically buzzing with each new fact she lays on the table. I reserve myself for what this dinner *should* be for: eating. Not trying to win over Baba. At the sight of no vegetables on my plate, Dadi takes authority and scoops some steamed broccoli onto it. When Alishba's not looking, I transfer them onto hers.

I reach for the fish, raking through it with my fork before scooping some into a napkin and shoving it into my pocket. That cat better be grateful. It's not every day you get to eat gourmet.

Baba reaches over and pats Alishba's head. "Good. Keep studying." If Alishba smiled any wider, her lips would tear apart. Seeing my siblings in constant battle is an exhausting experience. When we were younger, we used to all play football in the park, pretend to be explorers at our farmhouse, and take pictures at carnivals. And you might need to suspend your disbelief here, but at one point, Alishba and Ashar actually liked each other. Like normal siblings.

"Baba, I got a call from Uncle Tahir in the UK this morning," Ashar intercepts. "He's got my room ready now. It really is happening so quick, isn't it?"

Baba's eyes soften, a reaction that compels Alishba to clutch her trousers instead of jumping across the table and mauling Ashar for interrupting her moment. "Can't believe you're already eighteen and going to study abroad. Tomorrow, I might open my eyes and find you married."

"That's not possible." Ashar waves it off, a grin pinned to his face. "Dadi's for sure going to choose my wife, and you know how picky she is. It'll take her a hundred years to find my match."

Baba throws his head back, and they both erupt into laughter louder than Independence Day fireworks.

And that's when Dadi makes her big move, setting down her fork and clearing her throat. "Speaking of marriage, I think it's time we tell the children. Your baba plans to remarry."

The table falls silent like a butcher's chop.

"It's only been a year…" Ashar mumbles.

Alishba gapes. "Why didn't you say anything?"

"It's really *your* plan, Mama." Baba sighs, massaging his temples.

I'm frozen, gaze still piercing the fish bones on my plate, fork gripped so hard my knuckles pale.

"That's enough," Dadi says sharply. "That woman—"

She cuts herself off, breathing deeply. Her eyes flash as she turns to us. "Your mother is irresponsible, selfish and a stain on our family. The only way we can cleanse ourselves of her is for your baba to marry a woman who actually cares for our enterprise."

A scoff sputters out of my throat.

Dadi's head whips to me. "Amir?"

"A stain? Cleanse? Someone who cares for the *enterprise*? So Baba doesn't love this new woman. You just want to forget Mama ever existed. Even though she went *missing*. She needs us to find her—"

"She abandoned you all!" Dadi's fists slam against the table.

CHAPTER 3

The Interest of the Stronger

No one speaks.

Even the servants have frozen on the spot, mouths clamped. Ashar and Alishba dip their heads like they want to shut off their brains. Baba's face is blank, unreadable, but I don't miss how his grip tightens on the edge of the table.

The silence lasts a century before Baba sighs. "It's for the better of everyone, Amir. And we did try searching for her. Remember that it didn't work."

I still remember Baba's stricken face when he arrived home alone, Mama not by his side. They'd gone for an inspection of the brick kiln, ensuring everything was running smoothly. *"She was there one minute, and then gone. I'd just left to talk with the supervisors. But when I called out for her ... all that answered was the wind."*

Dadi said it was a set-up. That Mama wanted to go to the brick kiln because she'd have an easier time running away – out of the city with ears and eyes hired by us. All the police had to say was *"She ran away. She's an adult. She knows what she's doing."*

She's also my mother. The woman who raised me, taught me and loved me. At least that's what I thought. But every day she's away is another day that truth crumbles. Another day Ashar and Alishba flinch at the mention of her name. Another day I look at my reflection and hate it, wondering what wrong I committed for her to leave.

"I understand it will be a big change." Dadi sighs, wrinkly lips pursed. She's not louder than a pin drop, but her voice is imposing enough to lower everyone's gaze. "But we've waited long enough."

"No. Not yet." The words burst out of me before I think twice.

Dadi's engine of fury is about to rev again, but she plays along. "Is that so? Do you think your mother is going to magically appear? Your baba is going to be remarried by the end of summer. If she returns before then, that will be the only way this wedding is stopped."

Ashar and Alishba look to me, brows tilted, mouths in a tight line. They want me to laugh it off, smooth

Dadi's rage. But at the same time, I see that shimmer in their eyes. The need to *know*. They want me to find out ... want me to search for her.

I tap the napkin across my lips. "That seems reasonable."

And then Dadi lands her final blow. "You'll be studying at the farmhouse with Dada this summer, Amir."

The word *reasonable* now tastes like bile on my tongue. My lungs collapse. Each breath needles its way out of my throat. No. She can't do this. She's trying to get rid of me so that there's no way I can find Mama or stop the wedding—

"I'm not going." I squeeze my fork so hard it bends.

Baba tries to extinguish my flames. "There's just a lot going on this summer, Amir. We have to prepare Ashar for university abroad, and Alishba ... well, she's busy herself. The wedding arrangements are going to make the estate noisy and a hindrance for you. I think the farmhouse will do you good. Acres upon acres for horse riding. You know your dada was the best in his year back in the day? He'll teach you lots."

I can already hear Dada's sputtering smoker laugh echo in my ears. *"Faster, Amir! What, are you trying to win the race for slowest possible horse?"*

A shudder runs down my spine. "No—"

The doorbell rings. A servant steps to the side to answer it, but I move quicker. "I'll get it." Dadi's silent seething is enough for me to want to escape. My head is throbbing. I can't stand this food any more. Everything tastes bitter.

I pull open the door and a jitter of surprise shoots up my spine. It's Nani – my mama's mother. I haven't seen her in months. After what happened with Mama, she stopped coming around so often. But I have a feeling it wasn't her choice.

"Amir! Look at you. You've already grown taller since I last visited." If Nani wasn't holding a platter of sweets, she would've grabbed my cheeks and pinched hard. Although her smile is bright, it doesn't reach her dull eyes. Grey hair stringy under her orange dupatta, clothes worn and arms shaky, she's changed too. Less full of life, as though her internal batteries are blinking red.

"I thought you would be having dinner right now, so I brought some mithai for you all. There's rasgulla, laddu, gulab jamun and some patisa. How are Ashar and Alishba?"

I'm just about to grab the platter from her when a servant swoops in and takes it instead, voice gentle but firm. "Hello, madam, I'm afraid we're not seeing visitors right now. The family is busy."

Nani's smile falters; she rubs her hands. "Of course, I should know this. Sorry. Just wanted to check in on my grandchildren."

This is stupid. If Nani can't come in, I'll just go outside. I step out of the door and lie to the servant that I won't be longer than ten minutes.

We stroll around the gardens as the sun sets, and Nani's eyes soften. She used to feed the birds that bathed in the giant fountain, pick flowers and braid them into Alishba's hair, and chase Ashar and me around the camellia bushes. Those days were golden – when I was too young to understand the weight of my future; free, possibilities endless. But once Mama went missing, Dadi took over as the woman of the house. And that meant Nani had to go.

We sit on a bench embraced by daisies, watching fish swim lazily around the pond. Nani cradles my hand in her rough, calloused ones, and I do my best not to shrink down and cuddle up to her like in the past. Dadi might be watching with her hawk eyes.

I'm about to explode and tell her everything that went down at the dinner table when her words come first, smooth and soft like honey.

"You know, your mama used to talk about you a lot," Nani begins. But no matter how sweet she talks, she doesn't sugarcoat her words: *used to*. Even Nani has stopped pretending Mama is coming back. She was the one who first threw tantrums and demanded my baba hold search parties. But nothing came of them. A few months of repeated heartbreaks and now even Nani has given up. She talks about Mama as if she isn't missing but *dead*. I guess when you're a parent and you lose touch with your child, it feels like the same thing.

Nani smiles. "She would tell me that Ashar's become arrogant about being firstborn, while Alishba's competitiveness has taken her over. But *you*, Amir. She always laughed while telling me your most recent achievement. Even something as small as playing the right note on the sitar. She was so proud."

The words chip at my heart, especially after the remarriage conversation. No one will be able to see me as Mama did. I could let myself be free around her, as opposed to being a set of boxes on a checklist to everyone else.

"But you're not the same child any more, Amir. I'm worried for you."

It comes as a surprise, like sudden rainfall or finding a lost possession. No one ever voiced their worry about me. I'm the clever, spoiled, youngest son of a rich family. My inheritance is solid, my reputation maintains its prestige, and I don't have to worry about a single thing when my family makes every important decision for me. Some would even say I'd won destiny's lottery. To hear that Nani, of all people, is concerned about my future? It stings.

"You're wandering."

"Pardon?" I raise a brow.

Nani clicks her tongue. "Don't you at least want to *try* to become heir?"

"Too large a responsibility."

"But the blessings—"

"I can still get most by just being an executive."

"And what if you're a better fit than your siblings?"

"I could be. But that's a lot of extra work for a job that doesn't seem so much better. What am I getting out of becoming heir that would improve my life so drastically? What's the point?"

Nani quiets for a moment, releasing a sigh. Her grip on my hand loosens, and I know I've said something that didn't make it into her book of approval.

"Why do you think it's about *you*? And what you can get from it? A business is a service, a product – something that others need. It's not just family politics."

I shrug, slumping against the bench. Conversations

like this are a waste of time. I made up my mind. Seeing the way Ashar treats others to keep his position at the top, and Alishba's indifference to anything that isn't climbing up the ladder – I'd rather take a backseat and just accept what I'm given.

"Nani," I say flatly. "It's just pointless."

She doesn't look at me, doesn't even let out an amused hum at my words. Instead, she pats down her shalwar kameez and stands. "To whom? You? Don't you feel it, Amir – that invisible weight? Have you ever thought that your hands hold on to something more than your own future?"

I glance down at my hands. They're empty. She's spouting strange things again. I have to make things clear as day for her to understand. "I don't want it."

Nani looks at me and then to the waning sunset, her skin outlined in gold. "Everyone wants something," she says. "But not everyone realizes in time. I expected more from you."

I spring to my feet. She just pressed a button in my brain I didn't know was there. "You're just saying all this because if I become heir, you think I'll let you live in this estate again, don't you?" My chest heaves, up and down. "You're not any different from them. Ashar or Alishba or Dadi. All just greedy leeches."

Nani's face shatters, eyes wide and glassy. Her lips open and close as if to say something more, but a chorus of shouts slam against the northern gate. The guards rush forward. I stand to see what the commotion is. My eyes widen.

There's a mob rallying outside our estate.

CHAPTER 4

Cat Got Your Tongue

I never knew just how loud a crowd of thirty could be.

My ears are ringing, as if I'm sitting on the sidelines of a cricket match. But in reality, I'm squished against a net of guards, peeking around their arms and legs to catch sight of the ruckus past our estate gate. It's an angry tangle of limbs – fists raised in the air, spit flying, legs clambering to kick the iron walls. None of these people look local; their unkempt clothes and dirt-stained skin aren't shared by the residents who live in this neighbourhood, DHA Lahore.

DHA Lahore is one of those government-invested residential areas where all things new are developed. Modern infrastructure? Here. Techy businesses? Also here. Luxury conveniences? Can't find a better place than here. So when I see a woman with scruffy clothes that should've been turned to rags long ago, you can understand my surprise.

"Stop the expansion!" one man yells from the crowd, his skinny arm shaking as it shoots into the air. He's a skeleton walking – just thin skin strapped over bones.

"Where's my daughter?" a woman shouts, tears in her eyes.

"What's going on?"

Before I can ask that question, Ashar does, rushing out of the mansion despite the servants' best attempts to snag him back. Alishba isn't far behind. Wherever Ashar goes she follows, needing to make sure he doesn't escape her radar. When they notice the crowd, Ashar whistles, while Alishba's jaw drops.

It's only getting worse.

Half the guards have mobilized to keep us safe, encircling us like a pack of wolves. The others fight in a verbal battle with the mob, threatening to extract weapons. Everyone's screaming at the same time. I can barely make out what this commotion is even about.

It's Nani who connects the dots. Her head hangs low, lips pursed. "I read about this in the news. Your baba is expanding the brick kiln by demolishing the forest around it. But people are going missing."

Expansion? Demolition? But the word that sputters out of my lips is "Missing?"

Alishba tugs on Nani's sleeve. "What are you talking about?"

"I didn't think it was true. Well, I hoped it wasn't. But if my family members started to go missing while working at the kiln, I'd be angry too."

The noise shuts off like a lid. Time slows. I can hear my own breath. Suddenly, the uproar isn't just something to observe. It's become a mirror – an ugly, piercing mirror. There are parents banging at the walls, children crying and begging for their families, siblings with vicious glares and shark teeth. You're telling me that they're here, protesting, because their relatives have gone *missing* while working at Baba's brick kiln?

Missing, just like Mama.

It sounds like the type of story to make a splash on PTV news. If I'm thinking it, so is Baba. He comes rushing out with his suit in pristine condition, and I swear his hair has been groomed since I saw him at dinner. He strides past us to the guards, voice clipped and quiet. "Get them out of here quickly. We can't have this making headlines."

The guards propel forward at his demand, threats more aggressive. The horde shrinks back like an evaporating puddle.

Baba turns to us, spinning us back around towards the mansion. "Nothing to see here, bacho."

"You're expanding the kiln?" I creep next to him, ignoring the clawing sensation in my gut that wants to ask a different question.

"We got a new investor recently. They own the forest around the kiln. Now, with their permission to demolish it, we've been steadily growing."

So that's the reason business has been so good. The thing about kilns is that once the soil in the area has been excavated, new land needs to be pursued. For the longest time we'd heard the strangest things about that forest: haunted, echoing whispers, shadows lurking in its darkness. None of that poses a problem now that it'll be reduced to dust and whirring machines.

The words almost trip over themselves on the way out of my mouth. "A—and the people going missing?"

Baba waves a dismissive hand. "The poor are always going to come up with lies to get higher wages or extra money. They have no other skills at their disposal."

"Talk about a tough crowd." Ashar barks out a laugh.

I sneak glances at the mob as we trek back into the house. The frenzy of their bodies and the sadness welling in their eyes doesn't seem to stem from a simple demand like more money. The glare. The trembling fists. The tight line of their mouths as they back down but not without a fight. I can feel it. It's personal.

"Don't you think we should call the police?" Alishba asks, a whine at the edge of her voice. "I need to study, but they're making so much noise that I won't be able to focus."

Baba pats her on the shoulder. "Don't worry, beta, we'll handle it."

Nani doesn't take a step inside. She lingers at the door, wringing her hands. "I better go. Enjoy the mithai."

Baba turns, and for a second I think he'll invite her inside like old times, but Dadi's hawk instincts switch on, and she blazes into the corridor like the first flash of sun at dawn. Dadi never liked Nani, from extension of never liking Mama. Mama wasn't the bride she'd chosen. Not a daughter from a wealthy family who would raise their status even higher. Baba had to fight to marry Mama, or so the tale went. It's why, nowadays, Baba can't refuse anything Dadi demands of him. He was the one who wrestled to marry a poor girl who ran away in the end.

Baba glances from Dadi to Nani, releases an awkward chuckle, and bids her goodbye.

"Next time, Auntie," he says to her. This isn't the first time. Nor the second. He's been saying that ever since Mama went missing. *Next time* is code for "never happening".

I feel like I should say something, anything – we left off on a bad note and with a sour taste on my tongue. I want to ask Nani so much. About what Mama thought of me. About who Mama was when she was my age. And if Nani feels the same way about losing her daughter as I feel losing my mother. Also the fact that Baba will remarry if we don't find her, and that over the years she'll reduce to a speck of dust in everyone's memories. Some days, I can't even picture her entire face. It's blurry. But the words, just like always, get caught against the butterfly net in my throat.

I turn, trudging down the corridor as I shove my hands in my pockets. I recoil. It's *slimy*. I pull my hands away and take a sniff. Oh no. The fish. Oh *no*. The cat!

Leaping up the stairs two at a time, I narrowly dodge servants and skid around the corners. That cat seemed well-behaved, but anything with knives for nails shouldn't be left unattended for too long. Maybe it fell asleep? Last I saw it was ransacking my closet like a pirate plundering treasure. It'll be fine. Once it smells the pungent, nutritious, flavourful flecks of fish in my pocket, it won't be able to hide from me.

I shove the door of my room open and slam it behind me. The lock clicks. First thing I notice is how there's nothing to notice. Nothing out of place. My room is a rather large rectangle, fitted with medals from the activities my baba told me to join, books that my baba bought for me to study, and frames of scenic lands my baba wants me to own one day. There's not much of *me* in here. The things I do like – my storybooks, the horse figurine Mama gifted me for my fifth birthday, and the ridiculous carnival prizes Nani won for me years ago – are tucked away under my bed.

The only thing that needles my chest is the empty suitcase next to the door. Dadi must've ordered the servants to set it there during the commotion. Is she that desperate to get rid of me? Does she really think I'm going to pose a threat to this remarriage? I don't need to. It's fake. No love. No companionship. Just a contract with two signatures. It'll fall apart anyway.

I want to believe it, despite the squeeze that strangles my heart. The aching throb is almost audible amid how quiet and untouched everything is.

Did the cat escape? Not possible, the window's closed. Could it be hiding under the bed? Inside the closet? I'm just about to crouch down when I notice the bump beneath my blanket. I raise a brow. It's not a small bump. Unless this cat grew four times bigger while I was away, someone's pulling a prank on me.

"Kitty?" I whisper, lifting the blanket slowly.

It's no kitty.

I scramble back with a silent scream. Breath heavy, eyes wide, and the hairs on my arms prickling, I can't tell you what I'm staring at. The creature lounging in my bed is far from any furball.

It's a girl.

No normal girl. Glued to the wall, I hold my breath as the girl-creature awakens. Bright electric-blue hair tumbles down her shoulders like waves, and her skin is ivy green, smooth like porcelain. She's wearing a magenta Anarkali suit, beaded and glimmering like threaded starlight. Limbs sharp and thin, she stretches. But her resemblance to the cat only hits when her eyes flutter open and red orbs glimmer in the low light.

"You can't be…" I sputter. "There's no way."

She yawns wide. I gasp. A set of sharkish, jagged teeth line her mouth. And on second glance, there are two tiny pink horns on either side of her head.

I thought only uneducated people believe that superstitious nonsense.

The realization comes in waves. First the plummet of my stomach, then chills shuddering down my spine, to finally the scorching fever that threatens to bring me to my knees.

There's a jinn in my bed.

CHAPTER 5

Flames of Fate

I scramble to remember everything I know about jinn.

Ancient beings, lurking near abandoned sites and shadowy areas. The reason why mothers usher their children back inside after Maghrib prayer when the sun goes down – because that's when jinn roam freely. Nani used to say they belong to different tribes, each with distinct freakish abilities. And, just like the rumours mentioned, seemingly able to shift forms from human to animal.

I've always treated them like ghosts. Or goblins. Or even demons. The stuff of nightmares. *Not reality.*

Now there's one in front of me, yawning with teeth as sharp as daggers.

I surge towards my desk and snatch a letter opener, pointy end stretched in her direction. "Wh–who are you? What do you want?"

The jinn girl freezes, red eyes glued in my direction, mouth parted as if *I'm* the weird one. She scrambles back in my bed, blanket clutched to her chest. "You can see me?"

"I wish I couldn't."

She screams, kicking the blanket off and throwing one of *my* pillows at me. I duck. "Oh no. Was it because I fell asleep? This can't be happening. Summon cat form!" She taps her horns, eyes shut, brow furrowed. I wait for the magic to happen. But five awkward seconds later, she's still sitting there like a statue.

"Um, I don't think that worked."

She pops one eye open. "Well, this is embarrassing."

A shudder against my door almost makes me jump.

"Amir, sir? I heard a shout. Are you OK?"

One of the servants. Should I open the door? Have them call our local exorcist? Get them to lug in buckets of Zamzam water to dump on her? No. I can't. I'm the one who brought this cat home, even though it's clearly not as advertised.

"I'm fine," I grumble back, still pointing the letter opener her way. "I ... just shouted in victory after solving a question!"

"Was it because I fell asleep?" the jinn girl mumbles to herself as she slides off my bed. She cracks her neck in one horrid snap, then each of her fingers, and finally her back. I've never imagined what a jinn would look like before, but it wasn't her. Silky hair, slanted red cat eyes, and, on closer inspection, a thin tail with a ball of fur at the end flicks back and forth. The heavy jewellery dangling from her arms, ears and neck is embedded with glowing gems. I don't know the lifestyle of jinn, but she must live a pretty nice one.

She steps closer, floorboards creaking as her bare feet patter across it. "I guess you leave me with no other option."

"What?" I swallow.

Her red eyes flash. "I'll have to kill you."

Welp, here it is. I knew this moment would come one day. It's an essential part of being human: death. Isn't that what we're all waiting for anyway? From the second we're born, the only thing of certainty is our upcoming passing. There's no use in fighting what's inevitable. All my life, someone else drew the blueprint. And this moment isn't any different. *I wanted to find you, Mama*, I apologize to her. *But destiny had a different idea.*

"Just be quick, will you?"

Her pointy fingers reel back at my statement. "Wait, what? I was just joking!"

My eyes snap open, and I scramble back on my feet. It takes me a second to clear my throat. "So was I."

"You're a funny one." She laughs, and the sound is like pots and pans smashing together – a riotous firework that could make ears bleed. She may be joking, with her eyes creased like crescent moons and one hand slapping her knee, but that doesn't mean I'm going to lower my guard around her. The first thing anyone learns about jinn: they're tricksters.

I swallow my nerves, forcing my voice to steady. "You never answered my question. Who are you and what do you want?"

She skips closer until we're inches apart, grin smothering. I hold my breath.

"I'm Shamsa," she states, no differently than one would discuss how water is wet or grass is green. "I'm not from here. But you probably knew that already. I stumbled all the way from the jinn realm to the human world, and then I missed my train back. Maybe this is destiny's way of telling me you're here to help." Her eyes sparkle.

"Over my dead body."

She cocks her head. "You have a strange willingness to die."

I cough, flailing my arms to put enough distance between us so that I don't have to smell the smokiness off her. It's an odd mixture of fire and spice. Like tandoori chicken. "Why'd you come here anyway?"

"For the same reason most jinn do."

"To annoy humans?"

"For the sweets, silly! Gulab jamun, patisa, laddu… Jinn are willing to risk a lot for a taste of that goodness. But nobody was giving me any. I almost fainted from the hunger. And then I found you!"

I can't tell if all jinn have bricks for brains, or just her.

"This must be some kind of hallucination. I'm going to sleep," I grumble, walking past her. I throw the letter opener onto my desk. Jinn or not, she's no threat. Walking around in broad daylight is more dangerous than standing in a room with her.

She turns to me with a huff, lips pouty. "I'm being serious."

"And I'm serious about getting a good night's sleep. I have to wake up early for horse riding lessons, then pack for the farmhouse, and then listen to my tutor on call the entire ride there as he rambles about the quadratic formula for hours on end. I must be seeing things from the lack of sleep."

As I stretch my back, she stares open-mouthed, eyes shimmering. "You're thinking about equations?

When I'm telling you about destiny and adventure and a whole different dimension?"

"And?" I set my alarm.

"And the workers from your baba's brick kiln that are going missing?"

I flinch, head whipping in her direction. "What do you know about that?"

Shamsa hops onto the window ledge, smile spreading like billowing ink. "Same as you. It's pretty hard to miss the mob protesting outside your door. Aren't you curious about it?"

She's a strange one, this hallucination. Mama once showed me how to brew some calming tea that would help with insomnia. I wish I remembered the recipe. But since my mind has decided to play an intricate trick on me, I'll let it have its amusement. "If I were, what would even change?" My voice is an echo skipping across the room. "I'm not the oldest or even interested in the business. You talk about destiny, but mine's already set in stone."

Shamsa makes a sound of enquiry. "How so?"

I sigh, my arms falling to the side. Why am I bothering to explain? But the words rush out of me, in a tone more bitter than I intend. "Because each move of mine is carefully constructed. Every sentence that leaves my lips comes from the posh and proper schooling for rich kids. And my day is broken up into strict blocks of *bettering myself*. You're bleeding into my sleeping block, by the way."

"At least your parents care about you."

Is that what she's going to call it? "What are you saying?"

But again, she doesn't answer. Instead, she hops off the ledge and stomps towards me, grasping my hands in one fiery second. Hers are warm, burning, just like the spark in her eyes.

"This won't do. You need to come with me."

Close. Too close. I try to jerk away. But she's strong. It's like squirming against a wall of boulders. "Why would I do something so ridiculous?"

She squeezes tighter. "No one's destiny is set in stone. At least, I don't believe that. That's what I'm here to prove, actually. You've helped save me from starvation, so let me help you find what *you're* looking for."

The conviction in her voice hitches my breath, as if she's stealing the life away from me to give spirit to her words. It takes a moment to find my voice. "But I'm not looking for anything."

She grins. "Aren't you?"

"Everyone wants something. But not everyone realizes in time."

Nani's words. At first I rejected them, caught up in my own distaste for the family business and all the politics that come with it. But if she's lived this long, shouldn't there be some wisdom to her words? It might just be an inkling or a fool's hope or a very bad idea, but there *is* a little voice in my head shouting its wish. And maybe I'd put a lid on it long ago, but as I'm holding Shamsa's sweltering hands, the kettle inside me boils, desperate to erupt.

Yet when it does, the wish releases in a mere whisper, a tiny cinder in a mountain of ashes – it's a quiet plea, too unsure to truly take flight, but I grasp it before it disappears. It's the first thing I've ever wanted. And the first time I'm willing to chase it.

I want to find Mama.

Adrenaline shoots up my spine. I jerk away from Shamsa's grip, but she must've noticed the change in my expression. If her eyes were glittering before, now they're *gleaming*. "All right. There is something I want. But how do I know you're actually going to help instead of drag me down?" If there's anything I've learned about this jinn-cat-girl concoction, it's that she's not the sharpest tool in the shed.

She doesn't even look offended, which only makes me worry more. "I know plenty! I can name all the provinces in the Kagra Kingdom and recite ancient ghazals, and I also just learned how to cook rose-flavoured jalebi. Bet you can't do that."

A sigh shudders out of me before I even know it. "You're right. I can't. I'm such a loser."

"Don't worry about it." She giggles, elbowing me in the gut with her extremely pointy bones. "Shamsa's here to save the day. What are you looking for, anyway?"

My throat tightens. It feels too early to speak my wish aloud, like sending off a baby bird that doesn't yet know how to fly. But it's this girl. Shamsa. She stares at me like the entire universe is between us, crammed into the edges of my room. That even the moon hanging in the sky and the crickets chirping in the night are listening to me, willing to do everything in their power to make my wish come true.

"I want to find my mother. She went missing a year ago. No one has been able to locate her since."

I need to. Now more than ever. There'll be no end to Dadi's gloating if Baba remarries. And I'd hate to see another woman act like a mother to me, as if all it takes is a signature and pulling on a costume. I have until the end of summer. Two months. Bigger things have happened in less time. Criminal cases can reach a verdict in three weeks. The Olympics takes around two. So why can't I find Mama during summer break?

For once, Shamsa is quiet. Then she nods. As if there's nothing more to say. "Then let's go."

"Where?"

"To the jinn realm," she utters simply. "Think about it. You've tried searching for your mother here and came out with nothing. Maybe it's because she *isn't* here. She's in a different dimension."

It's radical, so far-fetched that a chuckle bubbles at the edge of my throat.

"You're joking," I scoff. "You don't even have human sweets in your realm, let alone humans themselves. Why would I ever step foot there?"

"We have many things." Shamsa smiles, her fang catching on the edge of her lip. "And plenty of them are missing humans. Aren't you seeing what I'm seeing? Missing mother. Missing brick workers. And yet, no evidence to their whereabouts. How does one disappear without a trace? By entering a different world. There must be a connection. And I believe it leads into the jinn realm."

My gut twists. This night is already nothing but eccentric. Here, with a cat-turned-jinn in front of me, what's the harm in checking? Maybe then I'll finally wake up from this weird dream.

"And how do we get there?" I mock. "A magic word? Walk into fire? Hit me on the back of my head?"

She clicks her tongue. "It's a lot more normal than you think. All we need to do is catch the train."

"A train?" I purse my lips, almost disappointed. "Seems anticlimactic. Can't you just, I don't know … use your fire powers to jet your way over?"

Shamsa pales, sputtering like a butterfly caught in a net. "About that. Ha-ha. I don't have fire powers."

My face pinches. "How can you call yourself a jinn if you can't summon fire?"

This time her cheeks flush, the little horns on either side of her head flashing. "I know! You think I don't hate myself for it? All my siblings can do cool fire tricks like string flames into sentences or make fireworks or boil entire rivers. But me? I just turn into a cat." She shifts from left to right. "That's pretty impressive, isn't it?"

Her eyes tell me if I don't answer acceptably, she's either going to sob or eat me alive.

None of those options sound particularly pleasing. A jinn without fire powers is like a samosa without filling. Contradictory. But despite my doubts, I try to prevent any waterworks. "Cats are … cool."

"I think so too." Quick as a blink, she's back to giggling. Shamsa hops onto the armchair next to my window, unlatching the bolt so the breeze curls into my room like a whisper.

Tomorrow I'll have to leave for the farmhouse. And before I know it, summer will be over. Not only will the sweltering heat evaporate but also my chances of finding Mama.

Shamsa is perched on the ledge. "The train leaves in an hour. Come on."

"This sounds like a fairy tale."

She grins. "Fairy tales are only as unreal as the power to make them true."

My head swirls with everything that went wrong today. Detention. Picking up this stray jinn-girl-cat. Baba announcing his remarriage. Snapping at Nani. Wondering if I'll ever see Mama again. And this bizarre opportunity that could potentially find me dead in a ditch within the next hour.

The words slip past my lips before I can stop them. "Why are you helping me?"

I *should* go to bed. I'll wake up and realize it was all a hallucination, and then I'll step into the back seat of my driver's car and whisked away to the farmhouse for two months, listening to my dada's unfunny jokes.

And Mama will still be gone. And I'll never know where she went or what happened to her.

All my life I've listened to *should*s. But what *could* I do if I listened to myself?

"You didn't have to give me those biscuits." Shamsa hums softly. "Yet you still did."

CHAPTER 6

Trainwrecked

On my tenth birthday, I almost drowned.

Dada's farmhouse was a spectacle, endless fields of dewy grass, streams and lakes shimmering in the distance, animals clamouring at dawn. The house itself was a towering stone pillar cradled by bright flowers, vines embracing its walls and keeping it safe. At one point, I felt no warmer than within it, memories full of hearty laughter, delicious meals, and dream-like mundanity. In those days, family felt like the word, the group of us strung together by the happiness of simplicity. Baba didn't worry about the business on his days off, and Mama would dismiss the chefs to make her own special dishes. Dadi would gather us around, my siblings and me, and tell us stories of Baba in his youth, chipping away the perfect image he used to create – because he was just a boy once too.

The days Dadi didn't feel like telling stories, she slept in her nook by the window, book resting across her eyes. We took the chance to explore the fields, nets and jars ready to catch bugs and fish. Mama warned us not to travel far; wild animals might make us their treat. We ignored her.

As we waddled through the streams, Ashar caught a fish like no other: a vivid red with electric-blue stripes, round fins, and shimmering scales; I'd later find out it was a gourami. Too quick for my siblings' slow fingers, they put me in charge of the chase, and I gladly followed. Leaping over stones, running alongside the river, I almost missed it when it swam into a great lake, mingling among hundreds of other fish. But I had to jump. That fish was mine. Its round eyes had called to me.

I leaped into the lake. I didn't know how to swim.

I thought by just reaching out, I could grab the fish and row myself to the surface. But the second I plummeted inside, a blitz of bright fish enveloped me. I couldn't feel my body. Dizzy, as if I were suspended mid-air, time forgotten. The water turned dark, like the sunlight bounced off the surface and couldn't trickle down to me. All I could see was that gourami, mouth opening and closing, until muffled shouts clamoured above. One second we were locking gazes, and the next I was pulled onto the grass by warm hands, hacking water out of my chest. Mama stared down at me, tears in her eyes.

"If I came a minute later, you'd have drowned, Amir."

I never touched water again.

Not the drinking kind, or the bath kind, but the water that settled in streams, lakes, or worse, seas and oceans. When the waves hurtled like tumbling boulders, or when I couldn't see the opposite shore, all my mind wandered back to was that dark lake, my drenched lungs, and the gourami with its swallowing eyes, lips parted as if whispering to me. And Mama. Mama sobbing for the next week, clutching me to sleep as if I might disintegrate into a thousand grains of sand if she didn't hold on tight. Her aquamarine pendant pressed against my cheek until it left a teardrop-shaped imprint.

That's how I feel right now.

I've taken a leap, and now I'm drowning – but this time, Mama isn't here to save me.

My eyes retreat to the window I just jumped out of. Three floors high. I've never done anything like this before. Maybe I can climb back up? Or sneak back in through the kitchens? The most rebellion I've displayed is refusing to do things. Refusing to play into my classmates' schemes. Refusing to let Baba remarry. Refusing to give up on finding Mama.

But never have I stepped forward to make the change myself.

"You said your destiny was set in stone." Shamsa's words trickle into an amused purr, her body having morphed easily and – I have to admit – impressively into her cat form. "But this proves it isn't."

My stomach flutters. "We'll see about that."

"We have to slip past the guards," Shamsa says, pawing at the pond, splashing around in it. I thought cats didn't like water.

Reluctantly, I stagger to my feet. At the edge of the garden, all I can see are the cobbled paths lined with dancing flowers and the stone shed near the fence surrounding the estate. There are two exits near by. North and east. But only one of them is really on the table. The north exit is still bombarded by protestors, guards on full alert as they march back and forth, in a yelling match with some of the ragged men. The east exit is a small one, and if you're not paying attention, most would miss it. It's just an aesthetic archway into the garden, where only two guards are posted.

The servant's bike instantly catches my eye. A rusted silver heap of junk, but it's our only way out of here. I'm sorry to whoever owns this. When I get back, I'll buy them something that isn't hanging by its hinges.

"Distract the guards," I tell Shamsa, hopping on the seat. She salutes a paw to her forehead. I swear there's a smile stretching across her face.

As I roll the bike towards the east exit, Shamsa patters ahead, meowing loudly. Shadows creep out from behind trees and bushes, joining her. My jaw hangs. In a span of seconds, she's acquired a mob of five cats, all of whom were hiding in my garden. Is that why our strawberries are always half chewed?

Her mob scampers forward, and for a second I think they're going to pounce, claws unsheathed. But then Shamsa nuzzles her head against the guard's leg. The same tactic she used on me… How many times has she done this?

The guard coos, crouching to pet her head. But then a second cat, a scraggy ginger missing one ear, snatches the walkie-talkie on his belt and zips into the patch of trees. He yelps, and the other guard bursts into chase. But the cat circus isn't done yet. Two others knock down the first guard, pelting him with face rubs. I'd be laughing if I wasn't trying so hard to stay invisible.

Now it's my turn. The gears screech as I roll the bike forward. Just what I needed to stay sneaky. Biting back a groan of my own, I nod to Shamsa as I slip past the guard. He's still fighting for breath among the mob of felines blanketing his head. Once I'm through, Shamsa lets the others finish the job, scurrying towards me and jumping into the basket at the front of the bike.

That's it. I've really done it now.

I've never been outside the estate at this late an hour. A part of me buzzes with what I'll find, wondering how different my city must dazzle at night. But the other part wraps two hands around my throat. What kind of people are lurking in the darkness? Or perhaps, what kind of *beings*?

I'm not sure exactly how I've plunged down this rabbit hole, but now even the light at the top of the pit has vanished. There's no turning back. My eyes glide to the cat licking her paw in the basket of the bike I just stole-borrowed. A literal cat is leading me to a realm of tricks and traps, and I'm following her. Willingly. Ashar would have a field day with this. And Alishba would use this as evidence as to why I'm not heir material. But part of this is for them. I'm going to find Mama. She's not going to be replaced.

Shamsa yelps as the bike jumps over a rock on the path, fur spiked straight.

It's been a few years since I've ridden a bike. We were taught as toddlers, just so that we could pretend to have some kind of normal, not-incredibly-wealthy childhood activity to do. But I feel like a newborn deer learning to walk. Zigzagging, shaky steering, and slowing down when I should speed up – the cyclist next to me yells a curse as he narrowly escapes ahead of me.

Once I'm out of the residential district, my lungs seize.

The colourful lights of Lahore flash past us. It all blurs – the dark, purplish sky, the zooming motorbikes, the startling neon store signs. Lahore traffic will make anyone's adrenaline spike. A bright green rickshaw plods ahead of us, so distracting I can barely see around it. Motorbikes slide right up, slipping through the crevices between cars as they cut through traffic. Shamsa's red eyes widen at the glittering, bright sight. Even though I'd prefer a smooth car ride over my wobbly bike manoeuvres, we'd probably take three times as long to reach the train station. I might be risking death by bike collapse, but at least I can squeeze between cars and slip past hordes of people.

Lahore Junction railway station is the largest railway station in Pakistan. It's literally a castle. And I mean *literally*. It's built in medieval English fashion with thick red walls and clock-faced turrets. A reflection of the British Raj's impact, both positive and negative, Baba says. Several decades later, it's still standing. I'm not sure if that's a good thing or a bad one.

When we enter, I feel like I've stepped into a different world.

Trains are new to me. I've always been confined in the safe embrace of a car. The first and only time we'd taken public transport was on a rickshaw, decorated in our honour for an event. Yes, there was no one else but Mama and my siblings and me in it, but people could *see* us. That's public, isn't it?

I didn't enjoy it then, and I don't now. Without a bodyguard, I feel naked and vulnerable. As darkness billows in the sky, shadowy figures lurch around the pillars. Tattered men hobble across the platforms. Rubbish litters the railway tracks, and the metal stairs whine every time someone climbs them. But that's not the worst part. There are beggars huddled in the dark corners, moaning and mumbling.

A shudder runs down my spine. Baba's told me

stories about the chuha, or rat children. Abandoned kids who are purposely harmed by criminal gangs to appear more pitiful. They have sloped skulls and narrow faces resembling rodents from the trauma. Baba says passing by one without offering them money is bad luck. But I can't linger longer than a second. The sight of them makes my gut churn.

The decrepit nature of the station is something I've only seen in dramas. Even the stink is indescribable. Commoner life has only been for observation, never to partake in. Baba would pick out a random person walking by, and their entire life story would be rattled off as if it were written on the back of his hand.

"You see that woman? She has a humpback because of slouching over sewing machines. She works at a sweatshop. I can tell because of the vacant gaze in her eyes – unfocused, as if she spent hours staring at a needle. And she has at least four kids. The weight of her grocery bags tells me so."

I remember being naive, believing he was pointing out her problems so we could figure out how to help her. Instead, he'd said it as a warning.

"She's an example of why we work hard, Amir. Somewhere along the line, she made a bad decision and is now suffering for it. Don't become like that."

Every time disinterest for becoming heir slips onto my face, he finds another person to compare us to. Another scapegoat. Another symbol of an alternative, horrible life.

I discard the bike in a corner of the station. Skittering towards the departure board, I don't see any trains running now. It's past midnight. Which would explain why there's barely anyone here, only a few crooked stragglers I have no desire to get close to. My gut lurches. Was this all a trap?

I force my voice to steady. "Do we need to buy tickets?"

Shamsa hops onto my shoulder. "Nope. We'll pay when we arrive at our destination."

"What's the train like?"

"It's confidential."

"You have no idea, do you?"

"Hey, I've used it before."

With each second that flies by, the twist in my gut tightens. *Mama could be there*, I remind myself, against every logical cell in my brain. *She could be in the terrifying realm of doom full of the very beings she and Nani warned me about.*

"This is ridiculous," I realize finally, pulling at my hair. "This has to be a hallucination. Did Ashar put something in my drink? Or maybe I haven't been sleeping as long as I should…"

"Relax," Shamsa purrs, zen on my shoulder. I can't tell if her tranquillity comes from wisdom or the fact that she probably doesn't spend more than two seconds on any of her thoughts.

"I can't do this. I don't know you. I don't know this world. I don't even know if what you're saying is true."

Shamsa prickles, finally sensing my seriousness. "I'm *trying* to help you. I'm your friend—"

My stomach plunges. "We're *not* friends. Y—you're a jinn!"

"Who can turn into a cat." She nuzzles into my shoulder for effect.

Before I can refute this, the lights of the station flicker on, carving gold circles into the ground. Mosquitos buzz around them. Whirring fills the air, and metal wheels screech as a navy train slows towards us.

I may never have stepped aboard a train, but I know they don't usually look this eccentric.

It's *old*. Ancient. Almost immortal. With coupling rods, chimneys and a golden frame. Shadows dance behind the windows, lights glowing red. When the train whistle blows, a puff of purple smoke billows into the air.

For the first time in my life, no one's here to tell me what to do. And I have no idea myself. *Great plan, Amir.*

But I don't have another one. Search parties, posters, headlines... The Rafiq Bricks Company has spent the last year in public turmoil after the disappearance of my mother. It's only natural for Dadi to want to start a new chapter by marrying Baba to some robotic woman who'd never say no to anything. I can change that. If I have to follow this jinn-cat-girl into her world of tricks and fire, then that's a risk I'll have to take.

"See? It's real." Shamsa leaps from my shoulder to the steps of the train, scampering aboard. "Now keep your hood on. *Low.*"

I step on after her, tugging the hood of my jacket over my head. There's an attendant waiting, hands clasped together, a wide smile fixed onto his face. He doesn't even blink. Just continues to stare. Black eyes against a paper-white face. Is he not allowed to speak or something?

I take a little more time staring at the peculiarities. The inside is made of dark varnished wood and violet velvet cushions, mosaic lanterns hanging from the roof, flickering crimson. The shadows from within the compartments chatter in voices too muffled for me to hear. The few people I do see have an edge to them, a crookedness, almost like their skins are old clothes that don't fit any more.

For a train, it's not too bad. Just odd. Are we sure this unscheduled train is even heading to the jinn realm?

I whisper my doubt in Shamsa's ears as we stumble down the carriage, trying to find an empty row of seats.

"Of course it is, silly. Don't you see all the jinn?"

What? Where? I turn around and all I see are the same strange people minding their own business, the smiley attendant grinning back at me.

But that's when we pass under a tunnel. Two seconds of darkness shroud the train, lanterns snuffing and shadows hanging heavy. When the light flashes back on, my breath catches in my throat.

They've turned into their true forms. All of them. Jinn.

Twisted nails, sharkish teeth, three eyes and hanging fangs, skin in every gaudy colour – I've stepped into a nightmare. The jinn reading a newspaper has ram horns that twist like spirals. The lady sipping chai has scales across her skin that shimmer iridescently as the lantern fire flickers. And the attendant's paper-pale face is now a dark charcoal, eyes bright hazel, but that morbid smile is the same – perhaps worse with the jagged teeth he sports.

"Don't stare." Shamsa giggles. "It's rude."

I whip my head around to see she's back in her jinn form too – electric-blue hair slipping out from beneath her hood, but the red of her eyes is bright and burning even in the low light. She plops down on a seat next to the window, humming happily.

Baba's voice echoes in my head. *Bad decisions.*

I only pray this isn't one.

CHAPTER 7

Seized in the Sand

"So what happened to her? Your mum?"

The hairs on my arms spike upright. It's been half an hour since this train departed. At least, I think so – the clock above the carriage door has five arms that spin in opposite directions. Shamsa's settled in comfortably, full from the platter of mithai she ordered and curled into a ball with her knees to her chest. Just like I imagine a cat would.

Of course she was going to ask. Why did I think she wouldn't? But when my lips part to mumble out a response, the words are lost. That's when it hits me. I've never told this story before. First, because I was ordered not to, and second, because nobody asked. Teachers, investors, uncles and aunts – all of them knew not to broach the touchy subject. Their sympathy came in the form of head pats and shoulder squeezes, tilted brows and "sorry" uttered under their breath. Back then, I preferred it. Hidden under the covers of my bed, the last thing I wanted was a nosy relative asking why my mother left. I feared trying to figure it out. Because what if I was part of the reason? What if I was the one who pushed her away?

The easy thing is not to ask. Or answer. It's to find Mama and put that squirming sensation in my stomach to rest.

"Just disappeared one day," I dismiss, refusing to meet the heat of her gaze. I feel like she'll burn my walls down and leave me exposed.

Shamsa offers a lopsided smile. "If you want me to help find her, I'm going to need more than that."

"How about we start with you?" Deflect. I've learned it from our press and media tutors. If you don't like what a reporter is asking, change the question. "You haven't told me anything about this realm and where she might possibly be."

Shamsa looks more than happy to entertain me. Scooting to the edge of her seat, she picks up utensils to help with her explanation. "The jinn realm is a mysterious place even to us jinn. Some might even say there are dimensions within dimensions. But a lot of us are scattered across islands." She picks up sugar packets and spreads them across the table between us. "One of those islands is where I'm from. And it's overseen by the Kagra Kingdom."

"Kingdom?" It sounds so ancient. "Do people try to stage coups?"

She taps her lip. "The last time someone did was three thousand years ago. So not too far back. But the Kagra family has kept succession tight. They have their own selection process to determine the next ruler."

"And what about all the missing people — how do they get here?" I think back to Mama.

"Well, haven't you ever heard the stories?" She cocks her head, smile flashing dangerously. We pass under a tunnel, and shadows dance over her face. "How a little kid wanders into a forest without ever being found again? Or adventure-seekers hiking up giant mountains mysteriously vanish? And what about the people who enter abandoned buildings hoping to escape the weather, only for their faces to make the human news days after? Where do you think they go?"

It sounds like a trick question. It sounds like Shamsa threw the fishing line, and now she's waiting for me to bite. I don't want to answer. Because I fear my answer will be worse than hers.

"There are many portals scattered across your world that dip into mine," she continues. "Several years back I heard about human miners who trickled into here and started an uprising at one of the most famous jinn hotels in the realm. You might not see the boundary that blends our two worlds, but you'll *feel* it."

A shudder runs down my spine. I think back to the farmhouse and its sparkling lakes. About how the second I slipped in I felt my senses lost to the water, its pressure pulling me further and further down. How the fish seemed too bright for my eyes, too interested in this new specimen that had entered their territory. Could I have crossed the line without even noticing?

"So you think my mother accidentally stumbled into the jinn realm?"

"Accidentally … purposefully … kidnapped." She says the last one quietly. "Anything could've happened. But one thing I know for sure is that humans often find themselves in the jinn realm. And all you need to know is where to look."

I scoot closer. "Where?"

She shifts in her seat, biting her lip. "Humans are… You're not going to like this. They're kind of like trash?"

My brow furrows. "What?"

"Not judging their personalities! Although yours does make me wonder if that's true too. But anyhoo, like trash, they float from place to place. Scraped away. Pushed to the margins. So all we have to do is look in those margins."

Hope crinkles in my heart. "You'll tell me where to go?"

Shamsa smiles, reaching over to place her warm hand atop my own. "I'll *show* you."

Silence hangs between us, our gazes suspended for an eternal second before the train screeches and jostles our hands apart.

"What's happening?" I mutter.

"You worry too much."

"Of course it seems like that when you don't have brain cells—" The words evaporate on my tongue as bright blue light filters in from the window. We're no longer passing under the night sky. When a fish swims near the glass and I catch the billowing tentacle of a giant squid in the distance, my stomach plunges to the floor.

We're underwater.

"Cool, right?" Shamsa giggles, clapping excitedly. "There's a portal beneath the sea that this train travels through to arrive in the jinn realm."

I can't breathe. My lungs have seized, frozen over like I've been dunked in ice water. The tips of my fingers are numb, grasping at the leather seat to steady myself. I can't remember how quickly I whipped my head away from the window, but the crick in my neck tells me it almost snapped.

"Amir?" Shamsa stands, brow raised in concern.

I don't have the energy or focus to answer. All I can do is shut my eyes. Drain this out. When my breathing is finally normal, the words that barrel out of my throat are hoarse. "You didn't tell me about this."

"The food? The red lighting? The train passing underwater?"

"Shamsa."

I feel her poke my arm. "Are you seasick? How's that possible?"

I can't tell her. Not because I'm afraid of her judging me – of course not, she's weirder than me anyway – but because I can't get the words out. If I open my mouth for more than three seconds, it's like I'm back at the farmhouse, underwater, darkness surrounding me, dragging me deeper until my lungs collapse.

"I need to go," I mutter. Sneaking a glance at the window, my gut churns as I notice the deep blue water shifting into a poisonous pink.

"Where?" Shamsa asks, tiptoeing closer to me. "We've almost arrived."

"Bathroom." I stagger to my feet, but everywhere feels like water, including the floor. Walls and colours merging like a painting, they swirl into a spiral that seems to suck the breath from my lungs. Three steps and my left hand shoots forward, grasping the edge of a table to keep steady. One jinn yelps as I accidentally knock over his drink. I don't know where I'm heading. Some lady gasps when my body slams into the side of her seat.

"Amir!" Shamsa's voice grows in concern. "Don't move."

It's too late. My body is fluid, flowing along with the current that pulls this train. Just like the first time I almost drowned, I can't control anything.

I smack face-first into something very solid. A low huff followed by pungent, acidic breath attacks me next. Glancing up blearily, I meet the raging gaze of a meaty, three-headed jinn.

"What's your problem?" His voice is liquid fire, burning my skin raw.

"*Move*," I urge. There's no helping my tone. All I want is air. Where can I find air?

"Picking a fight with me, brat?" he roars, shoving me back a few feet. My arm slams against a ledge, throbbing. There's a flutter of gasps and yelps as other passengers take notice.

A wave of bile rises up my throat. I clamp a hand over my mouth.

But he grabs the front of my shirt. Shamsa's distant yell echoes in my ear. He shoves me to the ground and pain blossoms all over. My head aches. Needles prickle down my spine. A groan oozes out of me.

The second I crank one eye open, I'm staring back at a sea of faces. Jinn hovering over me, on the edge of their seats, mouths wide and eyes wider.

"A human," someone gasps.

"A human!" the three-headed monstrosity yells. "Arrest him."

What?

The train honk drowns out the shocked commotion, blaring as the train shoots out from the water and sunlight floods past the windows. Another honk and the wheels screech to a stop. We've arrived.

I gasp for breath, inhaling like I haven't tasted air in years. Shamsa scampers up behind me, throwing the hood back over my head. She pulls me to my feet with frightening strength.

"Over here," a lady screams as uniformed jinn march onto the train. "There's a human!"

These burly men have tusks hanging out of their mouths, crimson jackets bright enough to blind me. One has elephant ears and the other is hunched over like a humpback whale. They rip me from Shamsa's grasp.

"Let go!" I squirm. But it's no use. They're two brick walls, and I'm nothing but a crumpled paper ball.

Jostled back and forth, I'm thrown off the train into… Is this sand? It's blue. But it feels like sand. Grainy, soft underneath me. Before I can even stagger to my feet, the officers pin me down. I hear the chains instead of seeing them.

"Hey!" I yell, finally returning to my senses. I don't know if it's because of the mouthful of blue sand I just chomped, but reality is hitting hard. "Do you even know who I am?"

The officers laugh. The sunlight is so harsh I can only see the outline of a station around us, and more freakish, crooked faces joining the watching crowd.

"You're nothing here, human," one officer says. Cold metal clinks around my wrists. "Illegal immigrants are sent straight to prison."

This is ridiculous. Nobody told me this. I wouldn't have come here if I'd known! He can send me back on that train for all I care. Nobody has ever treated me this way, like I'm scum beneath their shoe, about to get scraped off.

"Stop!" Shamsa breaks through the crowd. "You can't take him."

The officers laugh louder. "And who are you to tell us what to do?"

She pulls off her cloak. Long blue hair exposed, magenta Anarkali shining, pink horns glinting under the sunlight – the crowd gasps.

"The fourteenth princess and twenty-seventh in line for the throne. Shamsa Kagra," she announces. "And this human here is my servant."

I should've known. Silky fur and airhead tendencies can't hide the first fact anyone learns about jinn.

They're all tricksters.

CHAPTER 8

Walk of Shame

You thought you had bad nightmares? Try stepping into mine.

Arms pulled back in an aching hold, I'm chained up and shoved forward across the sand, surrounded by twisted officers and the princess of this very kingdom. If my predicament wasn't strange enough, the surroundings do their best to remind me.

A pale purple sky and a red sun lashing down with whips of heat. When I lick my lips, the air is salty *and* musty, like I'm tasting dirt dug from beneath the pink sea. Vast and glittering, the blushing water sparkles under the sunlight, shifting colours like a kaleidoscope.

They don't call it a kingdom for nothing.

Towers rise out of the sand like magical pillars, ancient bronze structures decorated with colourful crushed seashells. Dunes sweep in from the east and shower the city in cerulean sparkles, like we're in a desert globe instead of a snowy one. As we stumble closer to the ruckus, sandy roads evolve into mosaic tiles of different faces, some laughing heartily and others with furrowed brows, as if they're watching me from below. Jinn wearing loose, fluttering garments roam around the city, jewellery doing most of the talking – gold chains heavy around their necks and arms. Palm trees stretch over, shading lounging jinn as they thumb through beach reads.

If it weren't for the hordes of jinn roaming this place, it might not have been a bad spot for a weekend away.

"Keep walking," the officer grunts as he shoves me forward again, reminding me that I'm not on holiday. Heinous. I'd have him thrown in jail for this offence in my world.

"So what? Are you going to tie me to a stick and roast me over a fire?" I hiss to the girl next to me. Shamsa. The apparent princess of this kingdom. A fact she somehow forgot to tell me.

"Can't talk right now." At least she looks apologetic. Or is good at pretending to be. Fingers fidgeting with her collar, she still can't meet my eyes.

"*Really*, Shamsa? A princess? When were you going to drop this tiny, insignificant piece of information?"

She coughs into her fist. "We're nearing the royal ship *Shahi*. I'll explain everything there."

The *Shahi*? All I see are islands clustered together. One full of greenery and wild, ginormous plants. Another looks like a fisherman's dream – an amusement park full of fish-themed rides, stalls and restaurants. The third is shrouded in mist, speckled with small lakes, rivers and mountains. But then the fog clears, and I get a view of what stands at the centre of everything. My breath hitches.

A giant, castle-like ship is parked in the middle, pink flag waving as bright and high as the sun. It looks ancient, immortal; a constellation of wooden beams and mosaic pillars, intricate tapestries fluttering as sails, and cannons that could launch balls as big as boats.

"That's one big ship," I sputter.

She nods. "Not that it does much sailing – it's always parked here. Though parked might not be the best word... Think of it like a wedge," Shamsa explains. "You see all those waterfalls behind the capital island? Without the ship sitting where they intersect, the water would overflow and flood the islands. That ship's been acting like a dam for millennia now."

Flood? A shudder runs down my spine.

"And what's going to happen when we get there?" I ask.

Shamsa bites her lip, mumbling.

"I can't hear you."

Cheeks redder than burning coals, her words come out in a rush, as if hearing them all at once will somehow lessen the blow. "I'll have to make a case in front of the malik."

The malik? In front of the *king*?

This can't be happening. I'm Amir Rafiq, one of the richest kids in Pakistan. Yet here I am, in a different *dimension*, where no one knows the power of my family name. I'm covered in filth, my muscles are throbbing, and the royal guard of this cartoon kingdom is arresting me to be tried in front of their king. I've never wanted to sit down with a warm cup of chai more than in this moment. Especially since our cook knows exactly how I like it. Steeped in cardamom and with a sprinkle of pistachio.

"Keep moving." The guards usher us from behind, swords blazing with pink fire. We march across a glittering bridge, the mosaic path becoming more intricate, with pockets of wildflowers sprouting in between the tiles. Long, eel-like fish swim below us, scales rippling like a series of quick breaths. But that's not what makes me gasp. In front of me, more imposing than any aristocrat's mansion or politician's estate — and trust me, I've seen a lot of those — is the giant ship, hull fortified with blankets of moss, vines clawing up the decks and beams. The higher the floor the newer it looks — as if they forgot they could renovate what already exists. There must be a thousand levels, all full of terraces and lookout windows and fancy decks. Four minarets shoot into the sky like twisted candy, waving flags of a pink markhor, a screw-horned goat.

I have to hold my breath. It feels like I'm walking into magic.

It's strange. Usually people say that to see is to believe, right? But I feel the opposite. The more I see the more I can't believe it's all real. The gate is five iron doors deep. We enter a wooden hallway, framed with pictures of famous jinn royals. Or pirates. I can't tell the difference.

My awe dies down as we enter the throne room. It's so long it's practically a street. I can't even see the expressions on the faces at its far end. The throne looks like it'll grow two wings and hunt me down itself — giant metal feathers fan out of its back, embedded with jewels of every cut and colour.

The malik and malika are seated on twin thrones, crowded by advisers at their shoulders and other nobles mingling along the carpeted runway, laughing as they spot us. Some sit up in their chairs, eyes bright and eager.

My stomach does somersaults. I bet prisoners are a daily entertainment to these court folk. But humans? We're a rare treat. They're watching me like vultures, expecting a show.

"Your Majesty," one guard says. "Princess Shamsa has returned from the human world. And she's brought back a souvenir. A human boy."

Heckles skitter through the room. What's the best course of action here? Deny knowing her? Pretend I *am* some random human boy she plucked off the street? Run to the nearest window and fling myself out?

The malik groans as he sits upright. Even the malika finally takes interest, her amethyst eyes sliding from her manicured nails to me. "You told us your trip to the human world was for research. How is this boy a part of that?"

Research? What was she studying? The lives of Pakistan's most wealthy? The forgettable day of a boy who doesn't even make his own decisions?

It seems Shamsa didn't think this far. She flinches,

hair standing upright like a frightened kitten. When she speaks, her gaze lands everywhere but on me. "I … found him begging at the train station. So I decided to bring him here. Better a servant in the jinn realm than a beggar in the human one."

It's not a punch to the gut any more. It's a steamroller driving over me. She could've thrown me to the ground, kicked me, insulted my ancestors, and I still wouldn't be as shocked as I am right now.

"If you wanted to coddle humans, you could've picked up one of the many infesting our beaches," a jinn from the sidelines exclaims. He walks to the front, and I notice Shamsa's throat bob. He's orange-skinned, with arms like boulders and a jaw so long and pointed he could sword fight with it.

"Let her have some fun, Firas," a girl with a towering ponytail says, shovelling sweets down her mouth as servants rush to replace the platters. "She's just a little kid excited about her newest toy."

The throne room erupts into laughter. That's when I realize – the only people allowed to insult a royal would have to be royal themselves. The crowd jeering in the sidelines this entire time must be Shamsa's siblings, the other princes and princesses. There's got to be at least thirty of them.

However bubbly and carefree Shamsa seemed earlier, she's a tightly stretched elastic now, one word away from snapping. Her gaze zeroes in on the malik and malika, voice shaking with the effort to seem calm.

"I promise he won't be a nuisance. I'll keep him busy as my personal servant."

I almost choke on air. Where's my say in any of this? As I open my mouth to speak, Shamsa stomps on my foot. It takes every nerve in my body not to fold over and wail. *Never underestimate jinn strength*, I make a mental note. *Even if they're airheaded princesses.*

"I hope this won't act as another distraction for you." The malika twines her jagged fingers together, pruned lips pursed. "It's always *adventure* this, *dreams* that. And now here you are picking up strays."

"Actually, I think he'll be a big help." For the first time since the scene at the train station, she sneaks me a glance, lips curled into a small smile. I don't return it. My scowl is enough for her to shift away.

I'm just about to speak up when the doors to the throne room burst open, and another human is barrelled forward by an entourage of officers. He's thrown on his knees, bald head shining with sweat. "I didn't steal the mangos! I swear," he cries.

The malik waves a dismissive hand at me. "Go then, get settled back in quickly."

I don't even have time to react before I'm swept away. The rest of Shamsa's siblings boo at their entertainment being cut short, but are quick to turn their attention to the next human victim's trial.

"Make sure he gets an orientation!" the malika calls after us.

Shamsa's hand clamps on my wrist, pulling me out of the hall. I bite back a hiss. It's like being branded with an iron. "We need to talk," she whispers.

This is either going to be extremely amusing or utterly terrifying. At this point, I'm not sure I want either.

"That's my line," I grumble.

CHAPTER 9

Servant and Master

I'm talking to a princess.

Technically, I've talked to many. Pampered daughters of wealthy families, spoiled brats who've never been told no, and decorated girls who function as nothing more than pretty dolls. But I've never met a *jinn* princess. Here, in her giant room of wafting incenses and a thousand throw pillows, she doesn't look at me. Her gaze wanders over the wall, the windows, uncharacteristically quiet.

Is she waiting for me to kneel? To proclaim my service? To thank her for slipping me out of that situation and making me her servant? I know everyone needs their daily wistfullylookingoutofawindow moment, but it's been five minutes since we sprinted in here and slammed the door behind us.

"Sham—" I begin.

"I'm so sorry!" She spins around with a squeal, ivy skin flushed. "About everything. I knew that bringing a human into the Kagra Kingdom was illegal, but I planned to disguise you as a jinn. Except you started acting weird on the train, blowing your cover. I didn't know what to do. By the time I got to you, the train had already arrived and the crowd knew. The only way to save you from imprisonment was to expose myself as a princess and take you with me—"

I hold my hands high. "Whoa, slow down. One degree of nonsense at a time, please. Maybe start with why you declared that I'm your *servant*?" The word tastes like gravel in my mouth. I have to force myself to even say it. "Why not acquaintance? Or colleague?" Baba's used those words before – less than a friend, more than a stranger.

"You're right to feel angry." She flops down on the recliner at her window, cradling her tail to her chest like it's a comfort toy. "But there was no other way to save you. You may not know it, but humans aren't very welcome in this kingdom. There's no *friendship* with them."

Boy, do I know it. I tasted their hate for me when I got a mouthful of sand. I can even list off all the jibes the officers made on our trek here, but Shamsa isn't done with her dramatic princess monologue.

"I didn't mean for this to happen. I wasn't lying back in your room. I really do want to help you."

"Tell me why you were in the human world in the first place. The real reason."

Shamsa's lips tighten into a line. "You heard my parents. I went there for research. Because I needed an edge against my siblings. All of them are skilled and great at what they do, and then there's … well, me. I'm not someone they think is capable."

I think about my own siblings, both talented in their own ways – Ashar and his sociability, Alishba and her book smarts. A lot of people look at me, the youngest son, and don't expect much. All I have to do is listen to others, make little to no mistakes, and my future stays solid.

So I ask her, "Why does it matter what they think?"

"Because I want to be heir."

The world slows and zeroes down to the metre in between us. Her statement spikes a chord in my heart, one that I've never dared to strum. *Why?* is the question that pounds in my mind.

It doesn't make sense. *Why?* It's not going to change anything.

"Why?" The word finally releases, and it's nothing more than breath in humid air.

But Shamsa smiles, a careful twinge of her lips. Fangs hidden, red eyes glittering – it's the first time she's looked rather bashful. Her gaze slides from me back to the window, basking in the golden summer light that outlines her features like the strokes of a paintbrush.

"I made a promise," she says. "A promise to someone who saved my life."

She speaks no more. Because with Shamsa, nothing else needs to be said. Destiny, adventure, promises – all the makings of a children's fairy tale are the motives for her actions. She's a princess, so why would she not believe in fantasies? Even if she's a jinn, and her kingdom is a crooked one, magic simmers in her air. Not mine. My reality doesn't involve flaming sword fights or decrees of honour or the strings of destiny. It's survival of the fittest. It's a game of knocking everyone else down so you can stand at the top. The one thing that felt like magic in my life – Mama – disappeared. That's when I knew. Magic wasn't made for kids like me.

There's only one king in my world. Money.

Shamsa continues, brow furrowed with determination, tiny horns glinting. "You're smart, Amir. I saw all those trophies and awards in your bedroom. I'm not too shy to admit it: my siblings are clever. Much cleverer than I am. But with you at my side, I have a chance. With your help, I can become heir."

Funny. Those are the kinds of games God likes to play with me. I, Amir Rafiq, youngest son of the Rafiq Bricks Company, don't want to be the heir of my family's multimillion-dollar inheritance. But now this creature of nightmares, a jinn princess, wants me to help her win *hers*? Somewhere, my siblings are laughing at me now.

"You want me to stay your servant?" I laugh. This is ridiculous. "All in a game to outsmart your siblings and win the kingdom's favour? I knew you weren't the sharpest tool in the shed, but this is asking me to kick myself and smile at the pain."

"There's a reason."

I turn away. "Whatever promise it was, I don't think it's worth it."

"I do," she declares. "Because that's what a promise is. A bond between two people regardless of who they are or where they stand."

Bonds? I want to throw that word in the dirt and stomp on it. Bonds are bound to be broken. I saw that with Mama. She left us without a word. Even all the so-called friends I had before – really just rodents weaselling their way into my life for my connections, status and family wealth.

"Without bonds, without connecting to other people, a life stays grey. When I met you Amir, another colour was added." Shamsa giggles. "I already see things differently because of you. There's new hope, new ideas, new adventures."

My stomach stirs. Maybe it's because she's a princess, but I feel like a kid again, listening to Mama as she reads me a bedtime story. Naive, innocent, hopeful – I want to cradle her words and kiss them to sleep every night. I want to believe. I want to see things differently. But my heart's been broken enough that each time I try to glue it back together, it just falls apart.

"So you brought me here to help you become heir," I say, laying down order. She can sugar-coat and decorate, but I see her intentions plainly. Cats and jinn are sly creatures, and she's both. "You didn't care about helping me find my mother."

"I'm not going back on my word. I'm still going to help you find her, Amir. Think about it – with my connections, we can scour the entire kingdom." Shamsa smiles, and the sun glimmers against the angles of her face. She reaches a hand out to me. "Will you help me?"

Your baba is going to be remarried by the end of summer. If she returns before then, that will be the only way this wedding is stopped.

Dadi's warning. My mission.

"How does becoming heir work around here?"

Shamsa straightens, her voice taking on a serious tone. "It's a competition that lasts a month. There will be three different challenges that I'll need to pass. The final few royal children will then deliver speeches to the kingdom, and the subjects will decide who'll be their next heir."

A month. To find my mother. And to win this competition.

You can scold me later. Tell me I was a fool in the weeks to come. But right now, in this moment, I choose to believe that Mama, who went missing without a word, mysteriously vanished and is nowhere to be found, might be here. In this twisted realm of pink seas and purple skies, Mama could be waiting for me. I *have to* believe. Because if I don't, who else will?

And there's no one better than the girl in front of me to make me believe. The mortal enemy of a human, a *jinn*, wants to shake hands and work together. Never in my life would I have thought this possible. I should back out before I get swindled. They always have tricks up their sleeves – but I've already fallen for hers. And this girl isn't like other jinn. She can't control fire. She speaks of bonds, of destiny and promises and all the things I've long since abandoned. She speaks of a chance – to gain it all back.

If magic exists here, then why not Mama?

This might still be a trick. Shamsa did keep her identity and my fate on secure lock while luring me to do her bidding. I may be walking into an inferno that'll burn me alive. I have to make sure it won't. "I'll help you—"

Shamsa gasps into a grin.

"On the condition that you don't lie to me. No more secrets." I extend my hand.

She swallows her glee, maintaining a cool, professional smile. Her words burn as much as her touch when she grasps my hand. "No more secrets."

CHAPTER 10

From Riches to Rags

I should've said no.

That's the twentieth time I've had that thought today and it's only noon. Not only did I have to sleep in the same room as the other servants, it was on the cold hard floor with nothing but a thin straw sheet to blanket myself. The second I started dozing off, the first shy sunray fluttered through the round window, followed by a guard and his frog that croaked loud enough to wake even the demons in the underworld. I was rushed to the bathroom, rushed in the shower, and rushed to put on my drab working kurta. It's the colour of soggy newspaper. The fit? Frumpy. The details? Non-existent. It's criminal to walk outside with this on. The only solace about this entire ordeal is the fact that it's in the jinn realm. You couldn't catch me wearing these clothes in my world.

Despite all the classes and tutors and training I've gone through, there's one thing Baba didn't prepare me for. How to survive as a poor boy.

I haven't even remembered where I am by the time they get us working. First is foraging in the gardens, helping collect mushrooms and fruit for chefs to cook breakfast. The mushrooms are larger than my head and soft as a cloud; plush little stools that would make great furniture if they weren't edible. But the fruit is an entirely different story. I jump back with a yelp when a fist-sized red berry yawns to reveal a row of sharp teeth, pulp stuck between them like it's just ripped apart flesh. If I forget the traumatic sight of carnivorous fruit, then this part isn't so bad. With fresh flowers and the sunlight hitting my back, I can forget that I'm shackled into servitude.

But not so much when I'm pushed onto my hands and knees.

When we reach the hull of the ship, it's a haunted wasteland – labyrinths of rusting and creaky plumbing, rotting wood, flecks of ghostly apparitions flitting about. The stench of decay hangs in the air like the blade of a guillotine. How the *Shahi* is standing despite this being the foundation is beyond me. Each gruelling step I take is through swampy water, knee-deep, green and swimming with glowing fish I avoid at all costs.

Every few minutes, the largest pipes in the hull, big enough to be rooms of their own, gush with torpedoing water passing through. We all freeze when the hull trembles.

The head servant waves a hand. "Nothing to be afraid of. The *Shahi* acts as a sort of dam, directing different lines of water while also producing most of the kingdom's energy. You don't have to worry. The royals have kept it in a delicate balance for millennia without overworking it."

He then shoves a scrubber into my hands, ordering me to scrape the moss off the walls until I can see my reflection in them.

You've got to be joking. The audacity of these people! I'm a Rafiq. This is a chore only the pettiest of servants would perform—

"Not used to this, huh?" There's an amused scoff behind me.

I turn to see a human boy around my age. His hair is buzzed short and patchy in places. One glance and I know he's not worth my time – scrawny, eyes beady, lips pulled into a hungry smirk. We're the youngest two of our servant bunch, a mix of quiet humans and some jinn who avoid speaking to one another at all costs.

My first thought is to ignore. I may have signed up for servant duty, but not to entertain nobodies.

"You reek," the boy says, inching closer as he scrapes.

"Excuse me?"

"Of privilege."

A cold sweat forms on the back of my neck. I don't want people here to think I have ulterior motives. I'm just a mindless mule that does what he's told.

"What would I be doing here if I were privileged?" I retort.

"That's what doesn't make sense," he croons, shifting his entire focus to me. "You stand tall like you own this place instead of clean it, and your eyes say more than your mouth does. I can hear the words *I'm better than this* just from the glint in them."

Twelve years of posh schooling can do that to a kid. I can't suddenly transform into a forgettable speck of dust. All I can do in the moment is deny it. If *I* can't pull out evidence that I'm a hotshot rich boy, then there's no way he can either.

"Think what you want, but I'm just here to do my job." I force myself to keep scrubbing, moss peeling off the wood like old skin. There's no point in denying or accepting any accusations. If he wants to think I'm a rich kid, then I don't see how that's an insult.

"Mm-hmm," he hums, raising a scruffy brow like I couldn't have said something funnier. "You forgot to apply soap, by the way."

Heat prickles my cheeks.

At least lunchtime will let me catch my breath, right? Just a simple meal and quiet peace. I couldn't be more wrong. I should've rejected Shamsa's proposal before it even left her mouth.

Here I am, in the servant quarter of the *Shahi*, waddling in line to get my lunch. The splash that hits my face as the cook slaps a brown blob onto my plate strikes a shiver down my spine. *Inner peace*, I chant to myself. It's no five-course meal, but if I close my eyes and plug my ears, maybe I can pretend it's jelly.

The blob twitches.

Oh heck no. I slam my plate down at an empty table. Even if my appetite is vanquished, at least with no one to bother me, there's still some quiet to enjoy.

"Thought you'd got rid of me?"

Scratch quiet off too.

The boy from earlier sits before me, a devilish grin on his face. He has the same brown blob on his plate, but he shovels it into his mouth with glee, humming and grunting and licking his fingers with loud pops. "What? Is rich boy too scared of eating commoner food? Is your stomach so weak that you can't eat anything except premium-quality gold-flaked fruit from the Garden of Eden?"

He makes it so easy to want to strangle him. I stab my fork into the blob and tear off a piece, but when I raise it to my lips, my stomach screams. *Don't do this*, it tells me. *Please don't do this to me, Amir.*

The boy erupts into laughter. "The great young lord falls to the brown blob."

My cheeks flush. Fine, he can have this win. I slide my plate his way, and he hums with delight. We sit amid other servants and staff, who hastily inhale grub like it's their last meal. Maybe it is. Maybe I should eat the blob while I have the chance.

Fellow servants glance at us, no doubt sizing me up as the newest recruit. *Yes, I do hate it here*, I want to confirm as they raise a brow in my direction. Others are too busy carrying supplies and rushing through orders. I hear a few cooks shout in despair. "When is the fish shipment coming in? We can't make lunch for the royal family without it!"

"Apparently, the fishermen haven't caught any today. There's been a shortage," another says with a nervous bite to their lip.

I wonder about my own servants back home, and

if they wail in anguish if they can't find Alishba's favourite figs or the little umbrellas my baba likes to have in his mango lassis. The scruffy boy in front of me stays oblivious, the rest of the servants' worries flying over his patchy head as he engulfs bite after bite. Is his stomach made of titanium?

"What's your name?" I ask. If there's a chance I can report workplace nuisances, then I'll need to know more than his face.

"Yaqub," he offers easily. "You?"

A split-second idea to use a fake name crosses my mind, but he wouldn't know me anyway. There are thousands of boys with the same first name. "Amir. How can you eat that?"

It's almost impressive how he shovels that brown blob down his throat, no sign of sickness on his face.

Yaqub shrugs. "Don't get much food where I'm from."

That's when it occurs to me to ask. "How'd you get here?"

"I was offered a job here." He shrugs again, like he doesn't realize most jobs aren't in a completely different dimension. "My family is struggling. When I heard how much money was on the table, I jumped at the chance. Even if I can't see my family right now, I at least sleep well knowing they're getting dinner night after night as my wage gets sent back home."

Family. It seems I'm not the only one here for that reason. Our situations and reasons are vastly different, but I'm starting to feel like maybe this kid isn't all too bad.

"So, I hear you're the fourteenth princess's boyfriend?"

I spoke too soon. If I rolled my eyes any harder, they'd fall out of my head. "What are you on about?"

"You're not actually, right?" Yaqub snickers. When I don't respond, the smile slips off his face. "**Right?** Come on … please don't say you are. A girl that pretty with a heartless monster like you—"

"She's *not*," I grumble. "And may I remind you, *she's* the monster."

"Not in my eyes."

"I'm … her servant." It's even worse coming from my own mouth.

I don't get the chance to elaborate when another servant taps my shoulder. It's an orange-skinned girl with nails as long as knives. I almost jerk back.

"Amir, right? Princess Shamsa has called for you. Please meet her in the Gooseberry Garden," she says, seeming about as happy as I am. A scowl twists on her face, and I have an inkling it's because she has no idea how some random human kid got in the good graces of her princess. *Fed a stray cat*, I want to explain.

"I'll be there." If I can find it. First order of business: obtain a map.

Yaqub sputters. "Hey, you are telling the truth, right?"

"Sorry." I lift from my seat, sliding on a smirk at the last second. "Duty calls."

CHAPTER 11

Tricking the Tricksters

It takes an embarrassing amount of time to get to the Gooseberry Garden.

The *Shahi* sure does have a map, but what use is a map if everything moves on it? The colours twist and spiral like an optical illusion. Just when I think I'm moving in the right direction, I'll find the deck is at the opposite end from where I'm heading. And it's only ten minutes later that I realize the map can unfold like those paper fortune-tellers. By the time I finally reach my destination, my brain feels like an over-grilled fish.

"There you are."

Shamsa's sitting on a chair with three twisty legs, waving a jagged hand at me. The Gooseberry Garden isn't a garden at all. It's a sports field, grass so green I could burn my eyes looking at it, with seats lining the sides for an audience. Different weaponry and equipment hang from shelves at the back — arrows, cutlasses, cricket bats and polo sticks.

"Next time, just bring me with you," I grumble.

Shamsa hums. She's wearing a chest guard and a funny little leather glove. "So you're bad with directions, is that it?"

I'm not bad at anything. I just haven't really had the chance to use a map before. "You might not have heard of it, but we've got something called GPS where I'm from."

Shamsa giggles. "Are you really that smart, then? Or do you just have different technologies for different things?"

"Regretting your decision now?" I raise a brow.

She shakes her head, smile teasing. "Just curious about you and your world."

This isn't about me. She doesn't need to know what I get up to. They all start like that — approaching me to be friends, to play soccer, invite me for dinner. And then skitter back to me not a week later with a list of demands. "Our servant-master relationship is a temporary agreement. So let's keep it professional."

Shamsa puffs out her cheeks. "No fun."

I sigh. "Why are we here?"

"To talk competition. There are three characteristics that the kingdom looks for when choosing a new heir.

Physicality, artistry and diplomacy. Each challenge of the competition is going to test one of them."

I raise my brows. "You're telling me you need to paint pretty flowers to run a kingdom?"

Sounds pointless to me. It's baffling how rulers are supposed to be kind, beautiful, athletic and smart. It's like demanding a chef know how to ride a motorbike, or requiring a singer to be a black belt in karate.

She clicks her tongue. "It's about being **well-rounded**. And heir competitions only happen once every thousand or so years. People want a show."

That's one thing I'm glad we Rafiqs don't have to deal with. If I had to throw punches with Ashar or debate the value of different coloured bricks with Alishba in front of a live public audience, I'd renounce my name entirely.

"I just got word of the first challenge. It's archery." Shamsa points to a set of ring targets in the distance, colours like an optical illusion, as if they'd swallow any arrows that came near.

"The Kagra Kingdom's most beloved sport is archery," she says, nocking an arrow on her bow and pointing at me. I try not to flinch. "If the heir isn't good at it, then they don't have the concentration or aim to run the kingdom."

"So … just practise," I tell her simply, leaning back in the chair.

Shamsa's lips tighten into a wry smile. She lifts her bow and aims at one of the targets fifty metres away. The arrow flies, hitting the target just an inch from the centre.

I clear my throat. "Ah, I see you've practised."

"And yet, it's not enough." She shakes her head. "We don't do regular archery here. We do flame archery. *These* are the targets used in the game."

She turns to a basket of fist-sized balls, tapping them with a finger one by one. A green aura starts glowing around them, and they rise into the air. Each ball has a different coloured circular target on its surface. With the way they zoom across the sky at sharp angles and make erratic manoeuvres, I don't know how anyone is supposed to earn a point.

Her shoulders slump. "Other jinn can light up their arrows with flames and control their trajectory. But you know me… I don't have fire powers."

I didn't think it mattered this much. Back in the human realm, I teased her for it. But seeing the forced smile stretched across her face now, I realize I have no idea about the troubles she must've encountered because of it. A jinn who can't control fire … if it sounds ridiculous to a human, then jinn must have a field day mocking her for it.

"The flame archery competition is *tomorrow*. If I don't get at least a spot in the top fifteen, the kingdom won't even remember I exist."

"Tomorrow? Why didn't you tell me before—" I cut myself off. Of course. I just got here. She's putting me to work fast. "Let me see one of those."

She hands me the target. It seems like a regular hollow ball of metal and gloss. The only difference between each of the balls is the colour of the target ring. "Do the colours mean anything?"

"Colours are specific to each participant. The ones in pink paint are for me. If I hit any of the other coloured targets, I'll lose points."

Hm. Now that's at least something to muse over. I turn the targets over in my hands, pace back and forth, and then reach into Shamsa's quiver to pull out an arrow. When I brush the tip of it, a drop of blood inflates out of my finger. I glance from the arrow to the target and can't help the smile that spreads across my face.

"We do have different technology for different things," I say, "but you still need to know how to use them."

Shamsa cocks her head, little pink horns glinting against the red sunlight.

I tap my fingers against the ball target. "Can you get me an iron rod and some copper wires?"

"What for?"

"I need to try something."

"Which is?"

"Shamsa."

"Amir."

I sigh, levelling her goofy smile with my serious scowl. "You want to win this competition, right? Then you'll have to listen to me."

Shamsa clicks her tongue, disappointed. But even if I tried to explain what I'm about to do, it would fly straight over her sharp horns. She'd ask too many questions.

"Why should I trust a plan you won't even explain to me?" she asks, twirling a blue strand of hair around her finger.

My gaze flicks up, dry as a dead leaf. "You don't need to trust me. I trust myself enough to win it for you."

She bites her bottom lip, and I almost have the decency to apologize. It came out more stinging than I meant. But this is what I wanted, isn't it? A boundary. A line clear enough that she wouldn't try to cross it again. This is a transaction, not a friendship.

"All right," she surrenders, saluting one hand to her forehead. "I'll be back as soon as I can."

I watch her scurry away, tail flicking back and forth like a curious cat. While she's busy, I slide the phone out of my pocket. Right now, this hunk of metal is useless for communication. But I have different plans for it. Plying the back cover off, I pull out its battery.

Maybe this heir competition will be more fun than I thought.

CHAPTER 12

Straight to the Point

Want to risk your life to watch a competition? Look no further than flame archery.

It feels like the entire kingdom came to watch — fishermen from the harbour, restless jinn children at the end of a school day, tailors advertising their handwoven shalwars. The wealthy aristocrats and council members sit on elevated seats, shaded from the intense afternoon sun. Is that — no way — Yaqub's in the crowd too, holding up a sign cheering on Golnaz. Everyone roars, arms in the air, demanding a show.

I stand next to Shamsa. She's a shivering mess.

Her grip on the bow is so tight her knuckles pale. We're in the rear waiting area, and she's glancing from her siblings to the cheering crowd, biting her lip hard enough to draw blood. Each sibling is decked out in their chosen colours, from bright fuchsia sarees to navy-blue kurtas. I recognize a few from the throne room – Firas and his boulder-sized muscles are flexing for the crowd. "He's the third-born," Shamsa mumbles. "One flick of his finger and he can knock down a wall."

Then there's a jinn bouncing on her curly tail. Another unfolds their limbs like laundry, extending to a frightening three metres. But it's the jinn who walks in at this moment who earns the biggest reaction from Shamsa – hair made of smoke, billowing around her like a cloud, she walks like a ghost, hovering just an inch above the ground.

"Who's the apparition?"

Shamsa swallows hard. "That's Golnaz."

Her pale skin glistens like the moon, eyes a dark void and lips two unmoving lines. There's no humour in her face. I peek from Golnaz to Shamsa and can't help noticing that while Shamsa's focus is locked on her sister, Golnaz doesn't spare a glance as she drifts past us.

The siblings take turns wowing the crowd, shooting arrows with dramatic flair. Firas's arrow erupts into a firework that shimmers into a portrait of himself. He strikes a pose to match it. It's spectacle after spectacle – arrows that blaze into infernos; arrows that split into twin flames; arrows that burn and crumble into sparkling ashes. It's not easy for me to be impressed by jinn, but today they have my approval.

"Did you see that one?" I ask Shamsa.

But she's retreated to the corner, facing the wall, mumbling to herself. "You'll be fine. Even if they laugh, it's not like it'll replay in your head every day for the next five years. Ha-ha … of course not…"

Seeing Shamsa devolve into a nervous wreck feels wrong. As long as I've known her, worries haven't seemed to be a thing she possessed. As a scruffy cat, she trusted me to take her home. And even after waking in my room, she tried to convince me *I* was the strange one. What happened to the girl who's all sparkles and smiles?

I don't comfort people. Or, I'll admit, I don't know how to. It was Mama I ran to when Ashar used to call me names or when other rich brats teased me for being the last in line, the boy fated to never be heir even if he sleeps on a pile of fortune. She'd hug me tight, lips pressed to my hair, and whisper, *"But you're a great son to me. And sometimes, that's the most incredible thing of all."*

I'm not sure that'll work on Shamsa. Instead, I grab a glass of water and approach her, bringing the cool surface to her face. She spins around, flailing.

"Relax, will you? I thought you wanted this."

Shamsa takes the glass and gulps it down in three rapid beats. "I can't relax. If I lose, it's not just the heir competition I'll be forfeiting. It's my dignity too. And … the promise."

I roll my eyes when she's not looking. Talk about dramatic. But there's a shakiness to her gaze, like distant memories have hurtled to the surface and settled heavily on her shoulders. Whatever promise she made, I don't think it's the kind spoken in schoolyard sandboxes. But it's not my business to ask.

I hand her the quiver with her new-and-improved Amir-tinkered arrows. "Remember, *these* are your arrows. You have to use them for this to work. Just shoot like you normally would."

"OK." She slips on the strap and nods, eyes round and returning to hope. "I trust you."

She really shouldn't. Sure, trust in my smarts and my schemes. But not *me*. This relationship is as much a transaction for me as it is for her. Once this is over, I'll be demanding all the information she knows about my mother.

The booming voice that surrounds the compound wrenches everyone's attention. The host of the competition, a willowy jinn with gnarled arms like twisted tree roots, shouts into a levitating speaker. "Subjects of the Kagra Kingdom, are you ready to witness the royal flame archery competition? Let us welcome the malik and malika!"

The two rulers stroll out from behind a curtain, primly waving to the audience. The path lights up with fire, and for a second my heart jumps at the danger they're walking into, but then I remember: they're jinn. They strut through the fire like it's a fashion show.

The malik and malika sit above the host and pull out fancy binoculars. Looks like they do take this competition seriously.

"The rules are simple. Each royal child can only hit targets of their specific colour, and each hit on a target is worth ten points. A target is anything with painted rings that can move. If you hit a target that isn't yours, five points will be deducted. The fifteen royals with the greatest number of points will earn their spots for the next challenge! You have thirty minutes."

More than half the royal children will be out after this first challenge. We can't play nice.

Instantly, the ball-targets come to life, green auras glowing as they rise to the sky. I didn't know what to expect when it came to Shamsa's siblings, but it wasn't *this*. They're monsters, acrobats, and everything in between. A barrage of arrows zooms upward, and targets begin dropping like prices on Black Friday. Shamsa furrows her brow, realigning her arrows every half second as her pink targets flutter through the air like butterflies. Her hands shake, jerking back and forth, unsure if she'll hit them.

"Shoot," I tell her.

She glances at the target, then back to me. Pulling back, she lets an arrow fly. It's a gorgeous parabola and would've hit the target if it didn't swerve to the right. Then the left. Then zip upward. But just like that pesky ball, the arrow puts up its own chase. Despite the lack of flames, it's the arrow that pulls the target towards *it*, piercing it straight in the middle.

"It works!" Shamsa jumps in the air, squealing. "It works?"

I smile. "Thank me later."

It was a simple electromagnetic trick. The targets are metal, and so are the tips of the arrows. All I had to do was turn Shamsa's arrows into magnets, and they'd attract the targets to themselves. That's how my phone battery came in handy. The electrical current it possesses, paired with coiled copper wire, is enough to create my own magnetic field. Then it came down to charging each of the arrow tips so that they became magnets themselves.

The crowd cheers as more and more targets plunge. Shamsa's eyes burn with new-found determination. She quickly gains traction, bumping up the scoreboard with every shot. I hold my breath as I watch.

Firas is enjoying this, shouting in glee every time he lets another arrow fly. Instead of true aim, he focuses on explosive power, letting the arrows combust and take down the targets with them. He breaks a few targets that aren't his own, but with his wide range he racks up more points than he loses. Golnaz is another force to be reckoned with. She didn't seem like a threat at first — all ghastly presence and slow movements. But her arrows are quicker than a blink, spearing the targets before they even get a chance to move.

But Shamsa, despite all her airheadedness, is a good shot. The arrows do most of the magic, but the plan wouldn't work if her aim was off in the first place. My chest swells as she drops target after target. The points escalate. The crowd cheers. She reaches for another arrow—

And comes back empty.

Shamsa turns around. "Where are the arrows?"

I could've sworn I saw them in the basket behind her. But now, all of them, all hundred or so that I charged, are gone. Wait. I stomp towards a shadowy corner — they haven't disappeared, they're broken. Shafts smashed and split into pieces, tips torn off, fletching ripped apart… Someone did this.

I whip my head around at all the participants. There's not one face dripping with an ounce of guilt. Do jinn even feel guilt?

All the confidence Shamsa just sponged sputters out of her like a deflated balloon. She drops her bow, wry smile back in place. "Looks like there's nothing we can do now."

No. Nobody gets the best of me. "There's got to be another way."

Shamsa places a hand on my shoulder, gentle but burning to the touch. "You tried, Amir. I'm grateful for that."

I don't try. I *win*.

In my dictionary, attempts are just the beginning of the victory process. There's no end but *triumph*. When I try my hand at something, it's bound to succeed. Why do you think I haven't seriously run for heir of my baba's brick company? Because I don't want it. Because when I *do* want something, I put my entire heart and soul into it.

But I stop myself. Why do I want this? To find Mama of course. If I help Shamsa, she helps me. It's not the pout on her face that worries me. It's not the crowd's smiles turning into jeers that get my feet moving. It's not knowing that this moment is going to haunt her for ever that pushes my arm forward to grab the remaining pink paint.

"What are you doing?" she exclaims.

I dip a paintbrush in. "You're the one who said destiny isn't set in stone."

There's a spare wooden board. I stroke the paintbrush across it in three pink rings. Then I grab the board and make my way across the field.

Shamsa grabs my wrist. "You're not seriously thinking of—"

"Making myself the target?" I beckon, tossing spare arrows her way. "I am. The rules are that anything with rings on it that can move is a target. So aim for *me*."

Before she can refuse, I sprint down the field, biting back a hiss as flaming arrows soar above me. The crowd gasps. I can't let all my efforts go to waste. Shamsa is in the top twenty, but she's steadily slipping down the scoreboard without any magnetic arrows to shoot. She won't need them now. As long as I'm the target, I won't let her miss.

"Do it!" I yell.

Shamsa shakes her head, brows tilted. "No way."

I hate to admit that my plan has gone awry, and that it's not entirely my skills that'll win us this competition. It's her too. I need to rely on her for this to work, and she needs to hear it to believe it. "I trust you."

A grin erupts on her face.

I know she's a good shot. But I still can't help the clench in my gut or the sweat that trickles down my spine. *Please don't burn me alive... Please don't scorch my hair off... Please don't—*

The first arrow strikes the board dead centre. My eyes light up.

"Again!"

Shamsa's back to her determined state, arms forward, gaze steady. She shoots arrow after arrow, and I have to dig my heels into the dirt to keep myself standing. I sneak a glance at the fiery scoreboard with each royal's face in its flames. Shamsa slides up one spot, then another, then a few more until she's in the top fifteen. Three minutes left on the clock to make sure she stays there.

The other jinn have spotted me. Firas throws a tantrum, but the host says it's all within the rules. Even the crowd takes my side. If there's anyone that appreciates a good underhanded trick, it's a jinn.

"Amir!" Shamsa screams.

An arrow is flying my way. But it's not aimed at the board. It's aimed at my head.

I just barely catch sight of Golnaz's bow aimed in my direction before she turns away. Her grey arrow catapults towards me. Because of Shamsa's warning, I'm able to raise the board at the last second, catching her arrow.

"Negative five points to Golnaz!"

That's what she deserves.

A giant bell tolls darkly as the competition comes to a close. As I drop the board and glance up at the scores, a body tackles me. Rubbing the grass out of my face, I'm greeted by Shamsa's wide grin.

"We did it. I'm tenth place!" she exclaims. "It's a miracle!"

I slump backwards. I have a feeling I'm going to need more than a few miracles to survive this.

CHAPTER 13

The Gatekeeper

I'm a celebrity.

The flame archery competition is followed by a massive feast in the ship's dining hall. Twinkling chandeliers hang in the air, rotating like planets; sitars and pianos blast from the live orchestra; and crooked dancers sweep between tables, their jewellery clinking as they go. Butlers extend platters of glistening mithai, and my eyes widen. Didn't Shamsa say sweets from the human realm were rare to find here? But maybe royals don't have that problem. Shamsa's giddier than I've ever seen her, smile wide enough to break her cheekbones. Her eyes shimmer at every compliment, as if she's never heard a single one in her lifetime. And maybe she hasn't. Maybe she's always been the butt of the joke for not having fire powers. The realization strikes me with a burn in my gut.

We're friendless kids, Shamsa and I.

She's known as the incompetent princess, the one you should avoid to escape her plague of faults. While I'm the competent rich boy, so distrustful that the idea of friendship sickens me.

Shamsa introduces me as her guest, despite my clear human appearance and reputation as her servant. But to my surprise, the aristocrats, businesspeople, and fellow royals clap my back in delight.

"That was a good trick, I've got to admit."

I'm a spectacle. An exception. The night's MVP. Jinn stop to relay their admiration for my quick wits and devotion to Shamsa. Her siblings even ask which part of the human realm she found me in, as if deciding whether to pick out their own human servants too. But little do they know about our sneaky arrangement. I'm not a servant willing to risk my life for a princess I'm not even sure deserves to be heir. I don't work for her. I work *with* her.

I need to remind myself of it every second, especially when Shamsa finds me on a lone balcony, away from the party. She's flushed, eyes still glittering from the win. "Amir," she breathes.

I take a sip of whatever poisonous jinn concoction is the sweetest and tip my head her way. "Shamsa."

She leans against the railing, her blue hair dancing as a breeze picks up. "You trust me."

Is that a question? A statement? A tease she wants to rub in my face? "I only said so because you wouldn't shoot the arrow otherwise."

She hums, smile growing wider. "You can't take it back now."

I shake my head, ignoring her comment. "Shouldn't you be enjoying the party? Milking all the compliments you can get?"

"You brought me good news, so now I'll share some with you," Shamsa says. "Tomorrow we'll go down to the edges of the city. It's very crowded and dirty…"

I don't think Shamsa knows the definition of good news—

"But we'll start the search for your mother there."

My heart swells. I try to suppress the eagerness in my voice. "When?"

"Daybreak. Meet me at the stables."

I swallow the rest of my drink and allow myself a little smile. "I'll be there."

"I won't make you regret it." She giggles.

"Regret what?"

"Trusting me."

I practically skip back to the servants' quarter, humming while the moon shines through the windowpanes and lights my hair white. I snuck out a little napkin of treats when I left: rasgulla, gulab jamun and laddu. Because why the heck not? I'll just take a quick shower, slump down in my cot, and then tomorrow—

Yaqub sits on the steps to the courtyard, face angled to the moon. Shoulders hunched and brows tilted, he mirrors the quiet of the night – and the solemness of it too.

"Can't sleep?" I ask, leaning against the wall next to the steps.

"Did you have fun?" Yaqub shoots back. "Or was it just like every other fancy party you've attended?"

Ah. Another rich boy joke. This time, I play into it. "It was a bit below my expectations, actually. They didn't have a chocolate fountain."

"Do you always talk like that?"

"Like what?"

"Like a self-absorbed jerk."

I roll my eyes. Don't hate my vocabulary just because you don't have it. "I saw you at the competition. You were sitting in the audience holding up a Golnaz sign."

Yaqub scoffs. "Because that's all I'm good for."

"What are you on about?"

"I'm not like *you*, Amir. I'm not smart. I can't turn the tides of a competition at the last second. They were cheering for *you*, did you know that? No one expects anything of me. It's not fair. How am I supposed to compete with a kid who's probably had tutors since he was four?"

When did this become a competition between us? But Yaqub's not wrong. My first tutor did arrive on our doorstep when I was four. *"A few years too late,"* Baba had said.

I roll my eyes. "Go to sleep."

He shakes his head. "I can't. I keep having the same nightmare over and over again."

"Is it the brown blob?" I shudder. "Because it's the brown blob for me."

"It's when my family went bankrupt and lost all our money."

The temperature plunges. Yaqub stares out into the distance, fingers picking at the cuts on his skin.

"My baba once tried to start his own company. He borrowed some money, had the papers ready... We were all so excited. On the day of the launch, he bought us all kulfi, and we cheered for a future where we could eat as much as we liked, whenever we wanted. But it wasn't us who were going to do the eating. Other companies ate *us*. Baba had a funny word for it, just like that game… Ah, *monopoly*. He said it's when one company controls the entire trade of a product. And if they don't, they eliminate the competition."

I don't know why he's telling me this. I don't know if I want to stick around and listen.

"That's what happened to his company. To most new companies. Baba says Pakistan is full of corporations that have been around longer than some empires. And just like them, they pass their legacies on to their children, and the next, and the next. How is anyone supposed to compete when the same few ancient giants are blocking the door?"

He's not wrong. And because he isn't, I know this must be a true story. He wouldn't know all these details otherwise. I cross my arms. "There are ways to sneak past. You need to be—"

"Smart?" Yaqub spits out the word like it's poison. "Even if you're born intelligent, you need to go to school to hone it. You need support. Money. What happens to the people who don't have it?"

I've never felt the need for tutors. Every evaluation period they would tell my baba the same thing: *"Amir is gifted. He's excelling more than we expected. It's a born talent from him."*

But I've never stopped to think about the people who may *want* tutors. Or even basic schooling but can't afford the time or money. For once, I see an invisible line between Yaqub and me. One I didn't know existed.

Maybe Yaqub is smart. Or could've been. But there was a gatekeeper preventing him from reaching his potential: money.

"We went bankrupt." Yaqub releases a sigh, and a part of his soul seems to leave his body too. "I ended up having to work at a brick kiln."

My pulse gallops. A brick kiln? It can't be. I mean … there are probably hundreds of other brick companies. Who says he worked at Baba's?

"Their logo haunts my dreams sometimes. That stupid *R*."

Oh.

I'm sitting next to a kid who worked for my family business. And he doesn't know. He. Doesn't. Know. Another invisible line.

"I don't exactly remember how I got here. One day I signed a contract, and the next, I woke up on the shore of this jinn kingdom, grey sand clinging to my skin. I had the option of working at a construction site, a carnival, or the *Shahi*. Just the word *shahi* itself brought me here – *royal*."

He woke up on the shore... How many other humans did too? Was it the same coast that the train arrived on? Where's the bridge between the jinn realm and the human one? I need to do more digging. What if Mama stumbled here the same way?

Yaqub picks at a stain on his kurta. "Even if I'm a servant here, this is ten times better than the work I was doing before."

My throat bobs. I know there are rumours – people going missing and low pay. But you can find a way to complain about anything. I've been to the kiln. I've been to the corporate office. Admittedly not for long, but my baba's company is a good one. He wouldn't have so much support otherwise.

Yaqub doesn't agree. "I ... don't think I can go back, Amir," he says, voice cracking. "I want to do what you do. Make a difference."

The words puncture my gut and churn my insides. *Make a difference.* I wish I could pat his back and tell him that yes, that's exactly what I do, what purpose my life serves, the mission that I hope the rest of the world joins. But it's not true. I'm not sure what making a difference even means. Knowing? Outsmarting? Winning?

I can't tell him. I can't let him know that I'm the son of the man who owns the kiln he worked at. I can't say that I'm not the one who makes differences, and that someone else is pulling all the strings in my life. As Yaqub's gaze slides to me, lips trembling, all I can do is sit next to him and offer some sweets.

"Don't miss the brown blob now, do you?" I ask as he inhales a rasgulla.

He shakes his head, swiping at his eyes, while a hole burrows deep in my gut.

CHAPTER 14

To the Ends of the Realm

I'm not used to carriage rides.

Bugattis, Mercedes, Lamborghinis – they're sleek, smooth, and you can barely tell when they're moving. But this jinn carriage is a magical monstrosity. The windows are made from squirming vines that reach out and tickle you if you're sleeping. The walls are layers of leaves, some orange and brown and already peeling. And the light hanging between Shamsa and me is a globe of fireflies. When she wants them dimmer, she just taps the glass and their buzz dies down.

Every rock and pebble and measly crumb of dirt that the wooden wheels pass over shoots the carriage into the air like a rollercoaster. I'm glad I skipped out on that brown blob for breakfast, or it would've launched straight out of my stomach.

"And then we had a thousand kebabs we didn't

know what to do with," Shamsa exclaims, shaking her head at the memory. "And we're talking *giant* kebabs."

Remind me never to let the princess spin her own stories. She's been rambling for the entire ride about the time she asked the chefs for rhubarbs, and they misheard it as kebabs, cooking upward of a thousand. Somehow she thinks this is funny and that I'm amused. I assure you, there's not a smile on my face.

But she continues, eyes glittering at every second she recalls. "So what were we supposed to do with a thousand kebabs? We rode to the poorest town and gave them away, earning smiles in return." She giggles. "I begged my siblings to come with me, but they all thought I was wasting my time. Only Golnaz thought it was a great idea."

Golnaz? That eerie, ghastly girl who looks like she haunts a graveyard? I won't be able to forget the way she launched an arrow at my head. She doesn't sound like someone who'd give charity to the needy.

"You two were close?"

"Close?" Shamsa laughs. "I looked *up* to her."

"What about Golnaz is different to the others?"

Shamsa sniffles, lips twisting into a smile. "All my other siblings have amazing fire powers. But as you know, I'm no more unique than a human."

Ouch. But I nod, silently telling her to go on.

She pulls out a lighter from her pocket. I raise a brow. Why would Shamsa need one? But when she flicks it open and a small flame appears, my eyes widen. Within the fire is an image – a moving image. Shamsa is younger in it, hair short as opposed to the long waves it has today, but I recognize the tiny horns on her head, her giant red eyes, the way her cheeks gleam like soft buns as she cracks into a smile.

"It's a memory lighter," she explains. "It records moments in time."

A group of kids around her snap their fingers or clap their hands, flames summoned at their command. Shamsa joyfully attempts the same, but nothing comes of it. She tries again and again, and the more she does, the more her smile falters. The group of kids laugh and mock her, but one departs from the crowd to stand in front of Shamsa. It's a tall girl with swirling, smoky hair. Brow furrowed, she pulls Shamsa into her embrace, scolding the others. The flame of the lighter dissipates, and the memory ends.

"All I'm capable of is *this*." She taps her horns and shrinks down to a cat with a poof. Her tail curls protectively around herself. "Every year, I waited and waited. But the powers never came. Fire *burns* me,

Amir. Can you believe that? When they found out, they all laughed."

I shake my head. "I think it's cute."

Shamsa's cat ears straighten. "Cute doesn't make you heir."

"So she helped you?"

"As long as Golnaz had my back, no one dared to mock me. I can never repay her kindness. It might not seem like a lot to you, but not having fire powers as a jinn brands me a *freak*. As less than everyone else. Even my parents didn't look at me the same once they found out."

I shake my head. I can't imagine how Shamsa must've walked on eggshells around her own family. "I don't see you talking to her any more. What changed?"

Her gaze swoops to the vines across the carriage floor. "Golnaz did. After the heir competition was announced."

It brings me back to my own siblings. Despite his recent manipulative endeavours, Ashar used to treat me well. Take my side when Baba overworked me. Snuck me out to play football when he saw how much I hated the tutoring lessons.

Alishba was always soft at heart. She'd sigh a thousand times at the way I would purposely annoy her, as is the youngest sibling's duty, but when I did something wrong and was about to suffer Dadi's wrath, she took the blame on more than one occasion.

That's how I wanted to remember them. But everything changed when I turned ten. *Heir* joined my vocabulary. I heard it over and over – whispered between the gossiping servants, questioned by Baba's aristocrat friends when they came over for dinner, and of course by Dadi, who warned only one of us would survive.

"It's not your fault she changed," I tell Shamsa. "Cherish those memories instead."

Shamsa's eyes glitter, lips parted. "Do you do fun things with your siblings?"

"So many," I say. "Every Friday we played polo with the neighbours. For the Basant Festival, we'd work together to create a kite strong enough to fly. Never won though. Ashar didn't listen to me about which thread to buy. And on the hottest days of the summer, we'd visit our cousins in Karachi and head to Clifton Beach, kulfi in hand—" I clamp my mouth shut. My cheeks flush. I complained about Shamsa rambling, yet here I am.

But she doesn't seem annoyed. Her eyes are round with curiosity, nodding along. "How much kulfi, though?"

"Enough about me," I grumble.

She pouts. "You got to hear about my siblings."

"It's research for the competition."

"We're here, Princess," the driver calls from the front. As the carriage slows to a stop, my feet – finally mobile – slip onto plush sand. We're back in Fisherman's Bay, but the reunion only sparks sour feelings. No one wants to return to the place they were arrested.

Even now, the stares are piercing. Market-goers drop the fruits in their arms. Fishermen let their catches escape. There're so many jinn at this port, too many to even gulp down a breath of fresh air. Every one of them we pass on the sandy streets turns our way. *I get it. I'm a human. You all hate me.*

At least, that's what I think at first. But then it becomes clear that the stares sweep past me to Shamsa, their princess. She's like a butterfly in a field of moths, skipping around and waving cheerily. Some jinn approach to get a word in, but the bodyguards at each of her shoulders mean they'll have to scale mountains.

"Your Highness, sing for us again!" the crowd exclaims.

Another man waves his tattered cap in the air. "We miss the days you'd sing during the parades. Will you join the next one?"

It's all lost to the air. Shamsa tries to catch a glimpse over the shoulders of her bodyguards, but they usher us forward. Despite how quickly we're thrust past the crowd, she offers as big a smile as she can. They eat it up like fresh meat.

"We'd advise you to put your disguise on now, Princess," one of the bodyguards says. Shamsa pulls on the collar of her Anarkali, and the cloth extends like magic. She throws it over her head like a hood, and it instantly shadows her hair and face. Kala jadu as far as I'm concerned.

That's when I realize. Golnaz didn't cut her ties with Shamsa because she was incompetent. But because she was competition.

The kingdom loves her. Even with her faults and childish dreams, there's a sense of hope and magic she carries. It's contagious. Burly fishermen, exhausted from carrying buckets of fish, even turn to smile at her.

On the other hand, Golnaz is ghostly, freezing everybody with her gaze alone. She wasn't blessed with the easy comfort Shamsa provides. I could do something with this information ... but the competition is still what determines the heir. Shamsa may be loved, but that doesn't mean she's fit to rule.

And while Shamsa can only offer smiles, Golnaz has provided many other perks.

The entire capital is transformed into a city of revelry: carnival rides soar through the air, swimmers dance in the river that cuts through the town, and booths upon booths of games and food line the sparkling streets. Giant crabs are on display in cages across the markets, jinn children taking pictures next to them. It's a celebration of all things sea: rare fish hanging like prized paintings, jinn creating magic tricks as they mix fire and water. The music pounds in my ears, sitars and trumpets calling my name.

Bigger casinos, theatres, carnivals and amusement parks. Aqua shows with water dancers capture the crowds' attention, all with signs below that advertise: BROUGHT TO YOU BY ELEVENTH-BORN GOLNAZ. What she couldn't do with her presence, she's done with money.

But where did it all come from? "All these attractions … Golnaz is the one who set them up?"

"Sure did." Shamsa nods, looking almost proud. "She's provided the capital with so much entertainment it feels like every day is a party. Even when she was younger, Golnaz was interested in business ventures. How to develop things. Where she could improve them. I wish I was as smart and thoughtful as her."

Smart she definitely is, but thoughtful I'll have to wait and see. Didn't Yaqub mention earlier that among the many jobs he was offered here, one of them was to work at a carnival? Could it have been this one – Golnaz's?

But I don't get a chance to investigate. We move further away from the revelry, closer to the coast where the sand dulls into a grey. Pearly buildings shrink to rickety shacks, and the constant city commotion quietens to an eerie buzz. The bodyguards huddle closer to us.

Then I see them. The first human.

Just a scraggly man loading cargo onto a ship. This dock seems private – barren, quiet and dreary. The closer we get, the more humans I notice. Some of them are packing materials, others are hunched over, carrying tanks of gas and other cargo. My pulse gallops. I whip my head left and right. Where is Mama?

I shove past the bodyguards, barrelling towards the first human I can get close to. Mama's name sputters out of my mouth. "Habiba. Do you know where she is?"

The old man raises a scruffy brow, then returns to his work.

I rush to the next human, and the next, filtering through the crowd. But all I'm met with are shaking heads and muttered nos. By the time Shamsa and her guards catch up to me, I've made it to the end of the docks, Mama nowhere in sight.

"D–do you see her?" Shamsa questions. The water in the harbour swirls anxiously, almost mirroring the hesitance in her eyes.

"No," I huff. It felt so close – like reaching up at the moon only to realize it's really light years away. "Even here, she's missing."

"This is only the beginning of our search," she says, voice teetering between hopeful and afraid. The waves flip back and forth to match it. "There's really only a few areas in the Kagra Kingdom where humans roam. This is just one of them. Don't worry."

I was ready. To rub the truth in Dadi's face, bring Nani back, tell my siblings we weren't abandoned, and show my baba that Mama *does* love him, and that he made the right choice to marry her. It was all a misunderstanding. An accident. My mother is somewhere in this cruel realm. Dropping to my knees, I pull at my hair. A long groan escapes me.

Where are you? I want to scream. But a second question rings louder. *Why did you leave me?*

I kick the grey sand. Wait. Grey? Grey like the sand Yaqub mentioned when he first washed up on the shore.

My head cranes upward. Behind me are the docks, in front of me is the pink sea. But when I look closer, there's another island in the distance – full of tall, festering trees and shadowy flickers.

"What's that?" I ask Shamsa.

"One of the smaller islands around the kingdom. Probably empty," she explains.

"Are you sure?"

She shifts from one foot to the other. "As far as I know."

I can't wrench my gaze away from that ghastly island. The longer I stare, the more I think I'm hallucinating. Trees warp into twisting vines. The sea laps at its sandy shore like outstretched fingers. And for a moment – the barest split second – I think I see a shadow pass between the trees.

I can't give up now. I'll find her. I won't leave until I do.

Then the nausea overtakes me. That dark, paralysing sense of no control, like I'm falling into an abyss, drowning and breathless. Waves continue to lick the shores, edging closer to where I'm standing. But I can't move. I'm frozen when a giant wave curls above me, casting me in shadow, about to swallow me whole.

"Amir!" Shamsa yells, tackling me to the side. I shut my eyes before the wave comes crashing down on us.

But it never comes.

Blinking an eye open, I realize the sea has receded, barely inching onto the shore, almost as if it's scared to. No way. I saw that wave. It could've toppled boats.

I glance at Shamsa on top of me, wheezing from the rush. "Did you just…"

But she looks as confused as me. "Sometimes, I think the water listens."

CHAPTER 15

The Apple of My Eye

"Think, Amir."

That's what Mama used to tell me when I was stuck on a difficult maths question, or when she'd pause reading me a bedtime story to ask for my theories on what happens next, or when I'd beg her to tell me what she loved best about me – and she'd only laugh while threading her fingers in my hair.

Where could she be?

Almost a week has already passed since my escape from the Rafiq estate. Since then, I've boarded a jinn train, got arrested, been appointed a servant, won an archery competition, and found absolutely no lead to Mama. I don't want to admit it, but sometimes I try to imagine her smile, the way her eyes crinkled, or the scent that trailed in her wake – but I can't remember. She's slipping from my grasp with every minute that passes. All that shimmers in my memory is her aquamarine pendant, birthstone twinkling, pressed to my face when she hugged me close.

Baba had bought her many necklaces since, gold and studded with diamonds, but she'd only ever wear that one: the first one he'd gifted to her. *"Because it means something,"* she'd said. *"It means he believes in me."*

We're trudging back to the carriage when I ask Shamsa where else we might find humans in her realm. Where the margins are.

Shamsa flinches. It's the first time I've spoken in the last ten minutes. Her red eyes drag through the sand, looking anywhere but me. If I wasn't so strangled by my thoughts, I'd say she looks guilty. But it's not her fault. She didn't know Mama wouldn't be here either.

"They're mostly found near the docks," Shamsa says. "Kagra Kingdom's main harbours are for luxury ships and leisure boats – the docks for the workers are hidden away like that one, brimming with humans who regular jinn don't want to see."

"So humans are meant to be ignored here? Out of sight out of mind?"

Shamsa picks at her nails. "Generally … yes. Isn't it the same in your realm, where the worst of you are tucked away in places no one looks?"

My feet stumble in their tracks. I think of the brick company. How most of my informational visits to Baba's workplace were at the corporate office, air-conditioned and renovated for aristocrats. Despite the company being about bricks, I rarely saw the making of them – who worked on the moulds, how they were manufactured, or where they wound up.

"Right," I admit. "So where else can we find them?"

"The second type of human in the jinn realm would be someone like you: a servant at the *Shahi* or in a wealthy household. Human servants are a bit of a brag here – jinn enjoy showing off that they have control over the people who hate us."

My blood freezes, throat crackling dry. "Is that what you feel?" The second question sputters out of me before I even have a chance to think it through. "Did you think claiming a human servant would give you something to lord over your siblings?"

Hurt flashes across her eyes. She pulls away slightly, like the air around me burned her. My arm reaches out in advance of an apology, but I let it drop. We're not friends anyway. I help her, she helps me. And so far, I'm the only one who's got direct results.

"Of course not." Her eyes strain as she stretches on a smile. But it doesn't reach her ears. "As I was saying.

There are humans who work at the docks, as servants, as labourers, as well as those who care for nature – foraging, farming, agriculture. To be honest, there are so many places your mama could be."

My breath hitches. A memory floods over me, like warm soup on a frigid day. Mama and I strolling through the courtyard garden, her pointing at different flowers and telling me what they symbolize.

"A cactus represents endurance. Being strong in the face of everything." I remember how she tapped one of its thorns, giggling like it had tickled her instead of pricked her. *"And see all those magnolias? They represent nobility. It's why your dadi is always telling me to plant them."*

I had chuckled, imagining Dadi stuffing her nose with the pinkish-white flowers as if their magic might transfer to her. But as we strolled further, my stomach did a somersault. *"What about those?"* I pointed to orange flowers with crinkles at the edges, bright enough to rival the sun.

Mama hummed, ruffling my hair. *"Good choice. Those are irises. You give those to someone you admire."*

She has to be there. If there was any place she'd choose to be other than our home, it'd be where flowers sing. "Take me to the nature areas next—"

"Breaking news!" A jinn boy scurries around Fisherman's Bay, waving a roll of newspapers in the air. "Get your papers here. Tickets for the next challenge of the heir competition will sell out soon!"

"What?" Shamsa yelps. A bodyguard flags the kid down, and we're able to snag a newspaper. It reads "Royal Poetry Contest".

Shamsa's eyes widen. "Poetry? How come we didn't hear about this?"

I almost choke on air, clamping a hand over my mouth to prevent my laugh from slipping out. Shamsa, writing poetry? If the contest is aiming for amusement, then maybe this is a good idea.

"We've been out all day. They must've already announced it back at the *Shahi*." I suck in a breath. This must be the second challenge: artistry.

"Says here it's in *one week*."

Talk about a tight deadline. "Have you ever written a poem? Or read your siblings' poetry?"

"I don't have a talent for words, and most of my siblings don't either. Sometimes we're forced to present poetry during parades or festivals, but everyone gets ghostwriters to write for them anyway. It's never the skill of writing itself they're testing – it's the way you deliver the poem. A ruler has to be charismatic. Enchant an audience, capture their attention, and convince them of their words."

Finally, common sense has entered the conversation. It's a shame, though, not being able to see what tall tales and woeful rhymes she would've dreamed up.

Shamsa twiddles her fingers like she's shooting sparkles into the air. "We don't just read the poem, it's a complete performance. There'll be dancing, lighting, special effects. Whatever creative components we can bring to the table, the better. But you can count on me for that. The real problem here is finding a poet. Who you hire shows your influence. I've hired the same poet year after year, but he can't even *contend* with the other poets my siblings will be able to talk into writing for them."

Shamsa taps one of the bodyguards for a list, and he pops open a tiny briefcase, rummaging through endless items way larger than it should be able to hold. He could carry an entire kingdom's worth of documents in there. I guess he *does*. Finally, the burly jinn plucks out a thin ivory scroll.

"Look." She unfurls it, parchment reaching her lap. "These are all the notable poets in the Kagra Kingdom." Pointing to an insanely long name, she adds, "This is the one I've hired before. He's got a gift for alliteration, but that's not something most people care for. While Rayan here, he can dream up metaphors in his sleep."

I lean over. "So why not hire him?"

"That's the problem. My siblings always snatch the good poets first. It's a huge honour to ghostwrite for the competition, and especially for the royal children who've made a name for themselves. People don't ... they don't really know me. At least, not until now. Not until the flame archery competition. Not until *you* came along."

The sun must've shifted angles to shine directly on me because I'm burning. I thought I'd got used to Shamsa's bluntness, but never like this. My achievements ... celebrated? It feels like a fever dream. No matter how many stellar report cards, awards or medals were added to my collection back home, the response has always been the same: *More. You can do better.*

I clear my throat, snatching the list of poets from her. "OK, let's sift through our contenders. How about Neelam?"

"Taken. She only ever works with Hakeem."

"Hiba Zafar?"

"She favours Firas."

One by one, we go down the list, but every name is met with a dead end. I'm learning that although Shamsa is a recognizable face, no one takes her seriously. With fifteen left in the running, she's just one bee in the massive hive. She needs to become queen bee, and maybe that's a skill you have to be born with.

"What about this guy? Daniyal Kamraz."

Shamsa shakes her head, defeated. "He used to be a popular one – mesmerized the entire kingdom. But there's no way. He hasn't ghostwritten for years. No matter how many invitations he receives, he doesn't answer a single one. He's become some kind of recluse."

There's the crack of light – of possibility. Now I just need a hammer to smash it wide open.

"Do you have his address?"

Shamsa shrugs. "It should be in our books. But I don't know if he still lives there."

"Get in the carriage." I roll the scroll back up. "I know where we're having dinner."

Dinner shuts the door in our faces.

We're standing outside a lodge off the coast of the lake, across Fisherman's Bay. It's a scenic retreat: a lush forest at its rear, colourful wildflowers painting the ground, and a pink lake glittering under the late afternoon sun. My nose tickles from the spicy scent that puffs out of toadstools and glowing flowers. The trees make me question my eyes – as if they're growing backwards: branches and leaves thick on the base, but thinning out higher up the trunk. And the critters that flit between grassy crevices are playing games with me, tapping me on the shoulder only to disappear moments later.

I can see how a writer would wind up here, away from the world and its noise. If I had the time, I'd imagine taking a leisurely walk here with Mama, soaking it all in.

But we're not welcome. We knocked not once, not twice, but four times before a grim figure answered the door, not even polite enough to creep out from the darkness. We heard a grumbled "Don't bother me" from the shadows before the door was slammed in our faces. Shamsa had to sweet-talk the bodyguards to stop them from crashing down the wooden walls and demanding an audience.

"Daniyal? Sir?" I talk through the door. "We're … fans of your work. We'd really love to talk with you."

"I know she's the princess!" a nasal voice shouts from inside. "For the thousandth time, I'm *not* writing anyone's poem."

"But why?" Shamsa pleads, pressed against the door in mourning. "Your poems are loved by the entire kingdom. It would mean everything to hire you."

A scoff sputters. "Hire me? I don't want your money. Why don't you bring me a three-headed dog so I can keep the crows from picking at my garden? Then we have a deal."

"A three-headed dog?" Shamsa squeaks. "You can only find them near the volcanoes on the island of Ifrits. That's half a world away!"

"Then you have your answer."

Shamsa gapes. If I look closely, I'm afraid I might see steam wafting out of her head. "Don't sweat it. He wasn't going to say yes anyway."

"But … now what?" She sighs.

"Now we walk." It's far too nice here to let this scenery go to waste. It reminds me of our farmhouse back home: beautiful green trees, flowers, the birds chirping above. If I correct the colour palette, I can pretend I'm back skipping through those golden, simpler times. "A walk is a good way to scheme for new ideas."

Shamsa doesn't question it, perking up again like a kitten given catnip – and we walk.

She hums, I take in the surroundings. It might've been a nice little getaway were it not for the bodyguards who trail a few metres behind us, their gazes drilling holes into my back like I should be chained for even breathing next to the princess.

"Wow, look at those apples," Shamsa exclaims. "They're perfectly ripe!" She scurries over to the row of robust trees, glistening gold apples about to drop at the first rush of wind. Even I'm intrigued by their metallic sheen. How different might they taste from the apples back home? I reach up to pluck one.

"Don't touch that!" a high-pitched voice yells.

I whip my head around. Where did that come from? Is it the wind? I wouldn't be shocked if the wind could talk in the jinn realm. But then pain blooms over my shin. Something just kicked me. Jerking back, I see the runt with the anger issues: a little jinn girl with furrowed brow, her two pigtails flared up like spiked porcupines.

"I said, *no* touching."

"I wasn't going to eat it," I lie.

"Doesn't matter," she grinds out. Oof. Her teeth look sharp enough to mince my bones.

Shamsa pounces in, head cocked in wonder as always. "But these apples are ripe. You should pick them before they go bad."

"Mama's not here," the little tyrant mumbles under her breath. "Can't pick them without Mama."

I shake my head. "You don't need your mother to—"

"Yes, I do!" she argues.

"Where's your mother, then?"

She doesn't look at me. "With her new husband. The next time I get to see her is in three months."

The blaze in her eyes steals any objection from my lips. This isn't some kid pretending to be useless so her mama can do all the work. This is a bear cub trying to protect her den while her mother is away. It's in the huffing of her breath, the hunch of her shoulders, the clench of her fists.

I know because I've been this way too.

I pluck one golden apple off a branch and bite into it with a loud chomp.

Shamsa's eyes widen. "A–Amir."

The little girl growls, punching and kicking my legs. You'd think a kid pummelling me would hurt no more than the brush of petals against my skin, but she's a jinn. They must have iron knuckles and limitless power, because I'm one second away from becoming a prune – purple and bruised.

"Don't want me to eat it? Then pick them." I scoop down and lift the girl up, holding her next to the branches. She squirms before her gaze settles on a glistening apple. Reaching forward, she picks one, her breath caught in her throat.

"See? Was that so hard—"

Tears stream down the little girl's face. Oh no. Not the waterworks. Especially not when they erupt from little girls. I let her down and her fists fly to wipe her eyes, lips trembling. "Mama always picked the apples with me. But she's n–not here..." She hiccups. "I don't want to pick them without her."

When my mama went missing, a chain reaction unfolded. First it was hysteria – everyone mobilizing search parties and mourning her absence. Then it became spite – Dadi forcing the narrative of a runaway mother, manipulative and selfish. Nani pushed out of our house. My siblings and I protesting. Time ticking away. Hope fading. Resentment settling in.

I hated her for it. Whispers from all around me spoke of a penniless woman married into a wealthy family and taking it all for granted. That at the first flash of a challenge, Mama sprinted back into the alleys like a weak mouse. They whispered about her not being strong enough, smart enough, kind enough. That we Rafiqs are born different – and no poor village woman can carry the weight of the world like we do.

But I couldn't help it. Even when I shielded my heart from the things Mama loved to do, I realized

I was really shielding myself from the things I love too: reading the books she gifted me every year for my birthday because I enjoy the bizarre adventures in them; telling the gardener to plant petunias because they're her favourite flower, but also my favourite scent; feeding stray cats because Mama used to do the same, and because maybe I do find kittens cute.

Do they remind me of her? Yes. Does it hurt to be reminded? It does. But do I still love doing them? Absolutely.

I cross my arms. "I know that whenever you pick an apple, you remember your mama. And I know that it aches. I know that you're lonely without her. But that's why you *should* pick these apples, because that's when you feel closest to your mother. Pick them *because* you remember her. Pick them *to* remember her."

The little girl sniffles, rubbing the tears away. "But it hurts."

"I know." I swallow. *I know.* "But you're letting the world steal something special from you. Let apple picking stay special. When I feel alone, that's when I do these special things."

She eyes the golden apple in her hands, then looks at the branches heavy with more. She stretches out her arms to me.

I scoop her up again. She's silent as she plucks apple after apple. Shamsa watches her with tight lips, gaze flicking between me and the little one. But after we finish one tree, the girl chirps, "These brown spots mean a worm went through it. Mama taught me that."

And then, after another couple of apples, she pipes up again. "Mama said when you can blow an apple off a tree with one breath, that's when they're perfectly ripe." She begins blowing. It looks quite silly, and rather unscientific, but Shamsa and I join her, huffing and puffing like we're inflating balloons. Shamsa's enthusiasm devolves into a sputtering wheeze. I stifle a laugh. The little girl giggles. Within a few seconds, all our heads are thrown back, air dancing with our laughter.

"How did you do that?"

We freeze. Standing at the edge of the garden is a hunched, crooked man with hair like weeds, his one visible eye widened in shock.

Shamsa wraps her arms around the girl. "Strange man alert. Get behind me."

But the girl writhes away, giggles bouncing off the trees. "Baba!"

"Baba?" Shamsa and I utter.

"She's been quiet ever since my wife left me. Her light gone out. Like an empty lighthouse." The man ruffles her hair. "How did you get my daughter to smile?"

"A frown turned upside down is a smile," Shamsa says, eyes creased like crescent moons. "You can do that with a situation too."

"I guess you can," the man concurs, a smile snaking its way onto his own face. "I know I said I don't write for the royals any more … but I'll make an exception for you."

"*You're* Daniyal Kamraz?" I have to hold my chin so my jaw doesn't drop to the floor.

Shamsa jumps up and down, hair swimming through the air like waves. "Thank you. Thank you. Thank you."

He scratches the back of his head, shy from Shamsa's delight. "What's the theme?"

"Longing," she replies.

Daniyal smiles, gaze distant. "I know that all too well."

CHAPTER 16

That which is Born in Every Being

I've never liked parties.

Not banquets with pretentious aristocrats, nor galas for a charity no one really cares about – not even a casual cookies and chai. But *especially* not kingdom-wide festivals with a limitless budget. Bright, colourful balloons attack my eyes, heady street foods with their scrumptious scents tickle my nose, but the noise – oh dear, the noise – my ears are going to need a long hard rest after this.

The festival is a holiday for the entire kingdom, and they're enjoying it like a divine duty. Art exhibits are dotted around the streets like a beautiful scavenger hunt, while stages are blasting live music for everyone to enjoy. Closed-off roads have transformed into dance floors – bhangra, jhumar and kikli all clashing in one melting pot. Even martial artists have found their audience, performing kicks and flips, and chopping boards mid-air.

The only solace I have from all the ruckus is that I watch it from a balcony in the *Shahi*, awaiting the day's biggest event: the royal poem recital.

"Daniyal hasn't got back to me with my poem yet." Shamsa paces around the tearoom, where all the siblings and their ghost-poets sit in waiting. "He's not even *here*."

"It's a long ride," I try to assure her. "And you know what they say about writers. They'll rewrite entire books at the last second if they can."

"But what am I going to do if he's not…" Shamsa springs alert as the door to the room groans open. Her voice trails into a whisper when she sees who enters. "He's here."

Good. There's only an hour until the recital. He should've been here much earlier, and I'm not one to excuse tardiness, but if he's even half the poet Shamsa makes him out to be, none of this will matter: she'll shine tonight for sure.

But another jinn strolls in behind him. And she's not one to share the spotlight.

Golnaz is at his elbow, greeting her siblings with a dainty hand, as if already queen. Her smoky hair drifts behind her like a cloud as she introduces Daniyal to the room. Why is *she* introducing him? And why is he at *her* side?

But the confusion breaks in mere seconds.

"He's my ghost-poet for the evening," she says, lips curled in a faint smile.

Shamsa's jaw unhinges. A few minutes ago, she was a ball of nerves, and now it's as if everything that mattered has melted away, her eyes empty and heart hollow. She doesn't even question it. She doesn't even send a nasty look Daniyal's way. It's Golnaz she stares at, like a flame too bright or a painting too abstract. When it's Golnaz, she accepts defeat.

But I search for the answer. It doesn't take long to figure out why Daniyal's switched sides. One hand waves off praise while the other holds a leash … to a three-headed dog. If my memory isn't failing, he'd asked for one when Shamsa and I were at his door. But to think that was a serious request? And to think he'd abandon us for a prize after we got his tyrant of a daughter to shed her scowl – should I have expected anything else from a jinn?

"Royal children," an attendant at the front of the room announces. "Please be prepared to recite your poems in this order." He holds a sheet of paper aloft, then attaches it to the wall – retreating across the room to allow everyone to rush in. I drag Shamsa over to check the list. It's by age, which means she's one of the last kids to deliver a poem.

All I'm hearing is *time*. We have more time.

"Does it matter?" Shamsa huffs, back to her slouchy, curled-up ball of gloom. "We don't have a poet, and we don't have a poem."

It's true. There's no award-winning, metaphor-flinging wordsmith by our side. But I know someone who's won first place at debate club. Who makes a mean argument. Who talks little but says a lot. Who has a self-proclaimed *way with words*.

I pat her shoulder. "We have me."

Shamsa's tail flops to the ground. "This isn't the time for jokes."

"When do I tell jokes?"

She considers this, chewing on her bottom lip. "That's true. Are you sure?"

It's a gamble. As much as I don't want to admit it, poetry has never been my strongest suit. Novels are more my thing: grand worlds and thrilling adventures. But can poetry really be that different? What **is** poetry to be exact? Is it not just a confession of emotions? Because, as chilly as I can be, I do have those…

"Get the performance part ready. I'll give it to you when the time is near."

One by one, the royal children file out until it's just me in the room. I take a seat on one of the armchairs by the window, parchment resting on the table. I dab a feather quill into the inkpot. It's time.

I have a confession to make.

My lungs are about to collapse.

I'm running through the corridors, poem in hand – ink not yet dry from finishing just seconds earlier. The recital started half an hour ago. I could hear the *ooh*s and *aah*s from the window I wrote next to, but I blocked out anything past that.

I halt at the outskirts of the stage: a third-floor balcony of the ship overlooking the kingdom. The crowd is vast, jaws hanging as they watch the current performance. It's by Babak, a hoof-toed jinn who delivers his poem like a war epic, two others at his side blowing fire that twirl into different images – clashing cutlasses, a mother teary-eyed as her son joins the fight, and two lovers rejoicing at the end of it all.

So this is what Shamsa meant when she said the crowd demands a show. It's better than any theatre play I've witnessed. It's like a movie.

The next performance is even more fascinating. Seventeenth-born Sorousha describes the iconic landmarks of the Kagra Kingdom. The damp, earthy forests, the pungent and briny Fisherman's Bay, the spice and stickiness of the capital. As she weaves descriptions of each place, the jinn next to her stir bubbling terracotta pots, their smoke billowing into the crowd. My nose tickles as the fumes curl around me, and then I'm gasping at her innovation. I *smell* the salt and sliminess of the bay – as if I'm there.

It's sunset by the time Shamsa takes centre stage, and my nerves are now on edge. What did Shamsa prepare for the performance aspect? I've never seen that many beady eyes glancing upward, expectant and critical. Shamsa's older brother Bin is making his way back from the balcony, sweat pouring from his forehead. He looks like a glazed doughnut. Stage fright, maybe?

Shamsa's no better. Her head flinches left and right, refusing to look at the crowd. Fingers fidgeting with the collar of her suit, she looks like a deer in headlights, wishing to be anywhere but here. I skid towards the balcony, grabbing one knee with a wheeze as I hand her the poem.

"You scared the living flames out of me," she whines. "I didn't know if you'd make it in time."

"I don't know if it's good," I huff. "But it's the truth. It's my confession."

She takes the parchment with a curious gaze, chewing her bottom lip.

"Don't be nervous," I tell her. "You need to wow them—"

"I'm not nervous." She giggles. "I worried if you would make it in time, but now all that's left is a performance. And *that*, I can do."

I don't get a chance to ask her what she means. The attendant introduces Shamsa to the crowd as the twenty-seventh child, and maybe that archery competition did make news, because they cheer with sharp whistles and raise their fists in the air.

"Hi, everyone." Shamsa waves to the crowd, a rigid smile bolted onto her face. As she earns a few quips from the crowd, her shoulders relax, expression softening. I wonder how many times she's done this before.

"Today I'll be reading my poem, 'Long Lost'."

She clears her throat. I hold my breath.

In front of thousands
I stand alone, like a dark ship coasting an
endless sea,
Looking at the island that is you in the
distance.
You're sparkling. Radiant. Immeasurable,
But impossible to reach.

Time slows. Shamsa isn't just reciting the poem. She's *singing* it. Silvery, like chiming bells that echo across mountains. Birds perch on the balcony to listen. The wind calms to a subtle breeze, whisking her blue strands into the air. The crowd is silent, eyes glazed, lips parted – mesmerized. I can't blame them. My own expression is a mirror image.

Even the sea surrounding the *Shahi* seems to listen. With each word that leaves her, the water twists and the waves whirl, as if dancing. Normally, she's about as eloquent as a hyper puppy, rambling and easily distracted. Here, she stands like a lighthouse, and the crowd are boats she's prepared to guide.

Every day I think I get closer,
But you're still a spot in the ocean
And I'm still a scared, oblivious child.

I won't stop trying,
Because you're not just any island,
You're my homeland.
And I'm the sand on your shores
Inseparable.

She owned the poem. The crowd kept quiet, hanging off her every word. Even I couldn't help the way my jaw unwound, chest tight as Shamsa read my heart out to the world. For a second it felt like I'd offered myself up on a platter, open and vulnerable, but then I remembered that no one knows it's mine. In some ways, it isn't. Not any more. Not when I see the expressions in the crowd: tilted brows, shimmering eyes, *longing*. They've found a piece of themselves in it.

When the last word rolls off Shamsa's tongue, there's a moment of silence – of caught breaths and magic simmering in the air. Then the crowd roars in applause.

It's not the best poem. Not the most intricate, professional or complex.

But in the midst of all these tongue-tying, flowery royal poems, it's a breath of fresh air.

It's raw. It's real.

I clap for her too.

Thank you, Shamsa. For saying what I couldn't.

CHAPTER 17

Whispers under the Stars

Shamsa calls me back to her room.

The festival is still thriving, jinn breaking out into song and dance well into the night. Even my fellow servants were given a few hours of freedom, and most made a beeline for the cake stands and away from their brown blobs. Tonight everyone is celebrating, and when I walk through the door of Shamsa's room with my shoulders rolled back, I expect her to be too. We just won a top-ten spot, moving on to the last challenge. Instead, she's standing by the bay window, expression a mystery, soaked in a wash of moonlight.

"Sit," she says as the door creaks open.

Have the consecutive wins gone to her head? She's acting like a substitute teacher who tasted power for the first time. To ease the tension, I flop down at the edge of her bed, voice a drawl. "Are you really going to work me this late in the night? Is there a union here I can complain to?"

"Amir."

She says my name like a statement, but it also sounds like a question. With her back to me, I haven't a clue what she's thinking. From the way the walls are shrouded in darkness, I'm reminded of the time our roles were reversed – her in my room within the human realm, a fish out of water. Now I'm here, sitting on her bed, entirely within her power.

"Shamsa."

"There's something we need to settle." She clasps her hands behind her back.

I click my tongue, a yawn coiling out of me. "Can we do it in the morning?"

"No!" She turns around suddenly, face flushed and horns glinting. "I can't stop thinking about it. You wrote that poem about me, didn't you?"

I did? No, wait, hold on a minute. She thinks it's about *her*?

Shamsa's eyes glitter in the low light, flickering with uncertainty. What gave her that impression? That *presumption*? Oh, if Yaqub heard about this, he'd wring my neck like a washcloth.

But then it hits me, one of the last things I said as I handed her my poem:

"It's my confession."

I guess it's time to launch myself out of the window. The fire burning in the hearth must've hatched more flames because suddenly my cheeks are flaming. I jump off her bed lightning-quick, hands in the air like an accused criminal.

"I didn't mean for it to come off that—"

Shamsa covers her face with two hands. "I didn't expect this from you. It's quite a grand gesture."

"Look, I wasn't trying—"

Her hands drop, revealing sparkling red eyes and a coy smile. "What is it about me? My smile? My long, luscious hair?"

I drag a hand down my face. "Shamsa—"

She sticks a palm out to me like a stop sign. "But I'm sorry, Amir. You're a human and I'm a jinn. It's too complicated!"

I swat her hand away. "The poem was about my mother."

Her eyes widen. "Oh."

I flop back down on her bed, a rumbling sigh escaping my throat. "I didn't make it clear; it's my fault."

Shamsa pulls out my poem – my ghazal – from

her pocket, unfolding it. I could almost evaporate from embarrassment. "Explain yourself. When you wrote about 'looking at the island that is you in the distance' … what did you mean?"

I swallow. "I was referring to how my mama's smile used to be like a beacon, guiding lost ships like me."

"And 'you're still a spot in the ocean'?"

I clench my fists. I don't know why I'm telling her. If the recital laid my heart bare to the kingdom, now Shamsa's picking at it, trying to prise out every stitch that kept it closed. "I used to hate her, you know? And if I'm being honest, I still might. She was the glue of our household. The scale that balanced each clashing energy. With her gone, everything changed. Baba's moods. Dadi's strictness. Ashar's and Alishba's tunnel vision."

And my willingness to let others in.

"It's like the world was sucked of all its colours. Things that brought me joy I began to hate. And all the cruel looks and mocking jokes other kids sent my way just boiled my blood more. I only had one question the entire time: *why did she leave us?*" I cough out a chuckle. "Even now … I still don't know the answer."

Shamsa sits across from me, gaze dropping to the floor. "When it comes to people, change can't be stopped. All we can do is ask, but the answers are never obvious. I had to ask my sister too – Golnaz. Earlier this year, when the malik and malika announced there would be an heir competition, she stopped calling my name. No more afternoon chai, singing under the stars, long walks through the garden. I became completely non-existent to her."

"So suddenly?"

"When I finally cornered her in the library, she barely looked at me over the book in her hands. I begged her to explain, to tell me if I did something wrong. She just shook her head. *I'm entering the real world now. You're still stuck in your fantasies, Shamsa. I hate to be the one to break the news, but all the fairy tales and dreams and destiny you talk of? It's not real. It doesn't exist as far as ruling goes. And when I win that competition, it's because I knew the difference.*"

Even though I'm not the one her words were directed at, I'm burning, gasping for breath.

I hadn't thought about it before, but witnessing the glassiness of her eyes, I believe Shamsa has it worse than I do. Mama's disappearance was a physical rift; she was here one moment and gone the next. I might have more questions than Shamsa would, but Mama isn't able to answer. I can hold on to the hope that she doesn't hate me, that she never did. But Shamsa doesn't have that luxury. Every day, as Golnaz ignores her, she's reminded that their beautiful relationship will never return to what it was.

"Have you ever thought about giving up?" That's the only solution I see. Without Shamsa as competition, Golnaz won't have a reason to keep her away.

There's a moment of hesitation, a flash of something that sparkles in her eyes, but Shamsa shakes her head. Firm. "I want to be heir."

Here it is again. A wish I don't completely understand. Being the heir means shouldering a responsibility that wasn't yours in the first place. It means strapping on fake skin and performing for thousands. It means becoming a symbol, a figurehead, a poster person. It means saying goodbye to any life you thought was your own.

Maybe being heir is something ingrained in their lineage? An old jinn tradition I'll never understand? Even if I can't comprehend it, there's still something I do know: Shamsa's not cut out to run a kingdom.

I was raised to be a picture-perfect heir. And she's nothing like me. She follows trouble, takes interest in things apart from strict business, and jumps into reckless situations. If I were Shamsa, I'd take my freedom and run with it.

"Why?" I ask again.

"A part of me knows it's because by competing for heir, Golnaz has to acknowledge me again. She *sees* me. And even though it's not like we're skipping through the gardens hand in hand, it's better than cold indifference. She was the only sibling who cared, the only one who gave me attention. Can you imagine how stomped on I felt when I lost *her* too?"

I nod. I know how it feels to lose the one person who makes you feel real in the world. "But competing is one thing. You brought me here to help you *win*. Why do you want to?"

"A prom—"

"A promise. I know. But what about *you*? Remove everybody, everything else, all of it. Do *you* want it?" Stepping closer, I point at her chest. My voice comes out strangled, strained with desperation.

"You *can't* remove everything, Amir," she says softly. "That's what she told me, the person I made the promise to. I have to want it *because* of them. Everyone. Everything I can change. It's not about me. It's about what I can do."

I don't get it. I feel like I'm back in the courtyard bench on the day I escaped, Nani squeezing my shoulder as she sat next to me. Telling me there's an invisible weight in my hands.

My steps falter. Shamsa moves forward to catch me, one warm hand under my arm. She blinks once, her large round eyes sparkling. Then twice, and again until she's grinning at me like the sun as it pops over the horizon.

"We're going to find her, Amir. Then you can give her the poem in person."

We makes my stomach stir. I don't have the capacity for any more false friends. Some might think my walls are rock solid, impenetrable, but truly, they're made of glass. Every friend who's come and gone from my life has shattered it, and every time I pick up the scattered pieces, I find some missing. How many more will take from me without giving back?

I don't know if I'll have it in me. What do you say to the person who disappeared from your life like socks in a washing machine? What do you say to the one solid force in your life who melted like ice into water? I have so much to say and yet nothing at all. But all I know is that my own heart is shedding its cracked walls, pounding for the chance to see her again.

Words will come after.

CHAPTER 18

The Reason for Love

There was a time Mama used to tell me what she wanted.

We'd sit by the window in the dining room, overlooking the fields the gardener tended. Vibrant tomatoes, vines encasing the stone walls, wildflowers contained in neat little patches. The morning sun would brush its fingers through her hair and paint it golden.

"Why did you marry Baba?" I asked her, one bite into my apple.

I remember her laughing; a loud chorus like birds at dawn. It must've been a funny question, but I needed to know. Baba was out all day, and Mama was inside. The only times they saw each other were at dinner. Didn't she love him? Didn't she want to see him every second of the day, like I did Mama?

Her giggles lingered between us. "What do you know about love, Amir?"

I was even younger than I am now. "It's the thing that exists between us."

She ruffled my hair. "It exists everywhere. In the way the birds wake us in the morning. How the flowers bloom in spring. When laughter fills the room." Her smile burned brighter. "And sometimes, it's in the promises you make with each other."

"Promises?"

"A bond," she explained. "A contract between people that holds them responsible. When your baba and I got married, we signed a contract. But that's not the promise that led me to love him."

She didn't look at the ring on her finger. She looked through the window, across the fields, further than the horizon. "I come from people who don't have enough, Amir. Enough of anything. But your baba changed that for me, gave me more, much more than *enough*. And I told him I want that for more than just me. For others too. Your baba has the power to do that. And he promised me he would."

"That's why you fell in love with him?"

"That's why I fell in love with him."

I forgot to ask her then. Why she loved me. If she even did.

Did she make a promise to me too? Some unspoken

pledge the moment I was born? There are so many things I yearn to ask her.

But first, I must serve tea.

It's the only other scheduled task I have today, as a servant of the *Shahi*. Surprisingly, I've been getting better at chores. I now know the difference between soap and detergent. One is for your face and the other is for dishes. Right?

It's been a few days since the poetry challenge. I just finished scrubbing the millennia-old floorboards; I'm due for a change of clothes before I head to the tearoom. You don't want to know how much cologne it takes to mask the stench of wood that old.

As I enter the servants' quarter, there's rustling in the corner. Yaqub has a knapsack open, stuffing in whatever few belongings he has.

"Where are you going?" I ask.

He zips it up obnoxiously. "On to bigger and better things, rich boy."

"Enlighten me."

"There's a new job opening. South of here. New island that needs some help with construction. And get this: all the money I've earned in the four months working here, I can make in a few weeks there."

A part of me wants to tell him that we have it

easy here: servants in the *Shahi* still get hot meals, entertainment from our surroundings, and a warm (albeit stiff) bed to sleep on. The humans I've witnessed working on the docks seemed like they were hanging by hinges, minds elsewhere as their hands moved mechanically for them.

But the other part of me doesn't know how much money he needs. *"My family went bankrupt,"* I remember him saying. And that's how he wound up at the brick kiln. But shouldn't the wages be fair? Isn't the brick company providing each worker with enough pay for a decent life? Staring into Yaqub's flickering gaze, I realize it isn't.

"How much money do you need?" The words slip out before I know what I'm asking.

Yaqub raises an amused brow. "What? You're going to pull out your wallet and dish the bills out right now?"

"I … no." Even if I had brought my wallet to the jinn realm, that's not what I was asking. Yaqub realizes it too because he punches my gut with his next words.

"I want enough money that I can put toys in my sister's hands instead of a brick mould. Enough that my mama doesn't need to beg the neighbours for an extra cup of rice. Enough that my baba can take more than a half hour break in a day. Enough money to make a difference."

I swallow. "And going to this new place will give you that?"

"It's the closest I'll get." He smiles. "You could leave too, you know," he says with a pat on my shoulder. "I don't know what kind of deal you made with these devils, but if you haven't sold your soul completely, you should come with."

I can't. I have to help Shamsa. I mean, she has to help me find my mother. And it's not like I'm here to pay off a debt either.

"Happy for you." I clap him on the back. "But I've got to stay."

Yaqub rolls his eyes with a sigh. "Young love." He rips a piece of paper and scribbles something down with charred wood. "Here."

It's an address. "What for?"

"Just in case you start seeing sense." He scoffs. "You'll find me there."

It's my turn to roll my eyes. "I don't need—"

"Don't miss me too much." He's already waving, strolling off into the mid-afternoon sun.

I'm refilling Shamsa's cup of chai when she delivers the good news.

"You mentioned your mother might be interested in helping with foraging and agriculture," she says, an eager smile snaking its way onto her face. "I narrowed it down. There's only one place that allows human gardeners. Look."

She slips a pamphlet into my hands. It's an advertisement for a new, exclusive residential district in the western side of the capital. There are pictures of jinn families laughing, jinn couples embracing, jinn with smiles too wide for comfort.

"What am I supposed to be looking at?" I mutter.

"Right corner," she whispers.

THE BOTANICAL GARDENS
A JINN-CREDIBLE WALK IN THE PARK

"With it being new, they needed to find the cheapest and quickest labour. And that comes from humans."

My heart inflates like a balloon. "So she'll be there?"

Shamsa bites her lip. "We—"

But her words get cut short. We're all in the drawing room: several of the royal children, the malika, a couple of foreign guests from the next kingdom over, and of course my fellow servants and me, who dutifully offer refreshments. I was about to sneak a tart into my mouth when the door creaks open and the council files in, each of the ten members dragging their beards on the floor behind them.

They're the kingdom's most prized advisers, and they speak for the malik and malika when they can't be bothered to. Which seems to be often. I wonder if all royals get tired of the job after a certain point.

The member at the front is shaped like a chestnut, arms and legs like little stubs against his giant round belly. He clears his throat. "Congratulations to the royal children who have made it to this last challenge. The council's monthly debate is happening in a week. We discuss new undertakings, current affairs, and problem-solve ongoing conflicts. We have decided to open up our next debate to you children. And broadcast it to the kingdom. This is your chance to show us your ideas, abilities and suitability as heir."

Shamsa spits out her chai.

"The council debate?" she whispers to me. "That's all grown-up talk. Profits, debts, and what's that one thing my baba loves to collect? Ah, right, taxes."

I whisper back. "You're going to have to learn about it one day. Now's the chance."

"We'll be expecting interesting discussions. Out of the ten at the table, we'll be choosing the five best royal children to give their speeches during the heir ceremony. That's when the kingdom will decide." The council member finishes saying his piece, and everyone immediately dives for the mithai, swallowing down entire rasgullas. Are we sure the council members came for the announcement, or did they get a whiff of the sweets on their way to somewhere else?

Instantly, the room is buzzing, the royal children chugging down their chai as they scurry out the door. The girl with butterfly wings next to me mutters something about infrastructure, while a boy with a third eye on his chin rehearses in robotic fashion, "Vitality. Ingenuity. Prosperity. Those are the tenets of the Kagra Kingdom..."

"I have to prove myself here." Shamsa's lips tighten into a line and she pumps her fists. "One of the reasons people don't see me as a possible heir is because I'm young. If I can show them I'm serious, then I'm bound to sway some votes over to my side."

It's true. I don't see a serious bone in her body. Even now, with all the schemes and ploys in my book, I'm not sure if she'll win. Shamsa is ... a kid. A dreamer. She loves the people too much to be a realistic ruler.

But that's not for me to judge. I help her, she helps me: that's the deal. I don't care if this kingdom falls to ruin after I place her on the throne. Every ruler has their own legacy. I'm not sure if I'll stick around to find out Shamsa's.

That's when a lightbulb turns on in my head. "There's something we've been missing this entire time. We need an angle for you."

She raises a pointed brow. "An angle?"

"Your brand. What you stand for. Represent." I circle around her. "Now's the perfect chance to reinvent yourself in front of the kingdom."

She shifts uncomfortably, tail flopping. "But I like me. I don't want to be ... reinvented."

"You need it."

She mutters something in protest, but I've already descended into the depths of my thoughts. How can I sell Shamsa to be something more? Something greater than she is now?

I think back to the short moment at Fisherman's Bay, when the crowd surrounded her. They liked her already — despite her lack of fire powers or wits or trickery. And maybe that's it. She's the most *un*jinn-like jinn of them all. She doesn't work for deception. She works against it. She's a ... princess of the public.

I can already hear the crowd singing.

"Let's go."

Shamsa abruptly stops drumming her fingers against the wooden table. "Where?"

I flap the pamphlet in front of her. "To the public."

CHAPTER 19

Where the Scraps Go

Go big or go home.

That's another lesson I learned from Baba. When it comes to any competition, any investment, any battle, you put your all into it. Rafiqs aren't losers. If our thrones sit at the top, it's for a reason.

So I remind Shamsa that she's a princess. I have her order the shipwrights to build a custom carriage to ride around the kingdom in. It's bejewelled with the same electric blue as her hair, so that no one will mistake her presence. A banner waves from the top with her new slogan: SHAMSA: PRINCESS OF THE PUBLIC. HER TRICKS WORK IN YOUR FAVOUR.

The next morning, we roll into work with style.

Drawn by horses with horns and bat wings, the carriage captures the attention of anybody within a fifty-metre radius. Her velvet seat is cushioned and put on a pedestal so that the sunrays drop on her like a spotlight, and the driver, bodyguards and I become specks of grey in comparison. Pulling out the map, I follow the line Shamsa highlighted. We're not just parading the kingdom aimlessly – we're hitting the spots that matter most. The places Shamsa can make the biggest difference. Where her name will truly be established.

The slums.

The Kagra Kingdom is wealthy, but there's no place in the world where the rich can stay that the poor aren't hidden underneath.

Our first stop is an orphanage in a town that couldn't be further from the capital. Not just in distance, but in conditions. It's taken over by sand, the dunes towering high with jinn living in them. Curious bystanders slog through the grainy paths, watching as our carriage struggles through the shifting surface.

Even the toddlers haven't a lick of energy. They shelter themselves under what little shade the trees provide them, using sticks to draw pictures in the sand. It must've been hours since they started – their eyes say they've checked out of consciousness.

It's the matron who gasps when she notices the carriage pull in, like a star twinkling on a stormy night.

I tap Shamsa's shoulder. Time to commence Operation Captivation.

Shamsa lifts off her seat. When her lips part, a melody bellows across the streets.

The adults and children slowly turn in her direction, lurching towards her like cold creatures craving the warmth of a fire. Even though she's executing my plans, this operation is almost entirely dependent upon her. Does she have what it takes to enchant her people?

I believe so.

As her voice flutters through the sandy air and paints it golden, as time slows and everyone stares at her peacefully shut eyes, I remember the day she convinced me to dive in at the deep end with her.

If there's anyone who can captivate, it's Shamsa.

The orphans giggle. They clap in awe. They dance to the rhythm of her song. For the first time, the matron breaks into a smile, watching Shamsa like a divine offering.

But this is only part one of the plan. Shamsa finishes her song and clambers down from the carriage, letting each of her steps reverberate through the street, seizing any lingering attention. When she stands before the jinn kids, she has it all.

"I, Shamsa, the fourteenth princess of the Kagra Kingdom, want to extend my new charity efforts towards this orphanage. You will be the first benefactor of the Shamsa Fund."

I hand her the sack of jinn dinar we stored at the bottom of the carriage. It's from her own personal funds. A portion even came from the sale of her belongings. She pulls open the tie just as a breeze sweeps past. Money mingles with sand, and a tempest of cash flutters around the jinn children. Smiles pierce the dry air and cheers erupt on the streets.

"Shamsa!" they cry. "Princess of the Public!"

She glances back at me, beaming, eyes wide with wonder like she won the lottery and not these kids. I wink back.

We're just getting started.

Off to the hospices next; it doesn't take more than a smile and bubbly laughter for the jinn cronies to fall in love. She helps them onto flying carpets, feeds them steaming broth, and sings ancient songs as they clap and reminisce. Shamsa's natural gravity pulls people in. I'm almost at a loss for words, running to keep up with her whirlwind.

Watching her, something tugs at my chest. Is that what being a true heir looks like?

It wasn't like this for me. We were told smiles are a weapon, laughter is a contract, and tears are fuel.

Shamsa's bright beam of a smile rips me out of my thoughts. "Can we stay longer? I want to cook the grandmothers' favourite recipes that they can't make themselves any more. And exchange stories. And—"

"We won't have time." I shake my head, checking the list of places we need to hit. "The money is already a good offer." I hand her another bag of cash, and she passes it along to the caretakers, adding them to the Shamsa Fund. But I don't miss the way her gaze lingers on the people, hesitant to say goodbye.

The carriage rolls forward, money trailing off it as jinn cheer for Shamsa. It's incredible, really, how well our plan has worked. But it's even more surprising to see how happy Shamsa is. She hasn't stopped grinning – she's like the sun on a summer day.

"I didn't know I had it in me, Amir," she tells me as she waves to the crowd. "Thank you."

I turn to see her smile directed at me this time, and it's too bright, too pure. Even if she's the jinn and I'm the human. I clear my throat. "What for?"

"They love me. You made them love me."

No, I want to say. *You did that yourself.*

This mission was just a campaign around the

kingdom to give her an edge in the debate. But sitting next to her in the carriage, watching as hope fills the hearts of jinn everywhere, I realize it's so much more. We're opening the gates. Just like I thought with Yaqub, there's an invisible line between us and them, and we're helping to break it. There's no better person to embody that than Shamsa. She grabs abandoned dreams and hands them back to you. Makes you believe anything is possible. Golnaz can call her childish, but that's a power most people wish they had.

"Don't get comfortable just yet," I tell her instead. "We're not done."

She's forgetting the locations we're targeting serve a double purpose: finding Mama. We've seen plenty of humans already, pushed to the margins even in these slums.

So far, though, no luck. For a few, bone-rattling seconds, I'll think I see her dark hair or the curve of her nose, her beige human complexion … but it's always some other poor woman stuck here. It's only set off my nerves more.

Next on our route is the town from the pamphlet Shamsa showed me the other day.

It's straight out of a doll's house. Pristine. Perfect. Like it was built for fake people and not real ones.

Even the grass is crispy green, so sharp it looks like it'll cut me. We haven't stepped foot inside this posh neighbourhood, but the sign outside already tells me it's not for regular people. You have to take a *boat* to get in.

I want to turn back now. Take back everything I said. There has to be other places Mama can be, right? Why is the most likely place across this river in plastic town?

Shamsa is about to ask for a boat when she turns to me, eyes meaningful. "We can take the horses, if you want."

I meet her gaze and nod, gratefully.

We unhitch the horses from the carriage and leave it parked on the side of the street; it won't be as much of a spectacle in a place like this, where it's competing with every other shiny thing. The horses walk us over the bridge that leads into this immaculate town. Gates ahead block our path. A little jinn man waves to us from the booth attached, like we're getting tickets to the best movie of the decade.

"ID?" His squeaky voice rings in my ears. "Or do you have a resident's card?"

Shamsa raises her hand – the ring on her middle finger speaks for the both of us. A golden band in the shape of a crown, with a ruby signet at the centre. The little man jumps into a yelp before cranking the gates open. "My apologies, Princess, enter as you please."

We stroll through, and the air tastes different.

The buildings don't look real: walls smooth and spotless like they've been enchanted to look like silk. The patches of flowers that line the cobbled roads are so manicured I wonder if someone took a nail file to the petals. Even the sun seems bigger than usual, the perfect red spot in the purple sky.

Jinn mill about, each one of them looking the part on this almost theatrical stage. They don't wear what most jinn do – kurtas and salwar kameezes – but rather sport button-down shirts and bow ties, slicked hair and formal trousers. It's like I've been transported into a 1950s' TV show. Kids play on swings as their mothers chat with one another on the park bench. Fathers watch, hands in their pockets, fully set in their dad stances.

It's a dream. It's unsettling. Especially when I think of the neighbourhoods we just came from – right outside the walls of this enchanted place.

"Are you sure it's OK to be travelling without your bodyguards?" I ask Shamsa when we dismount the horses.

Shamsa giggles, waving a hand. "Of course. This is one of the most secure places in the capital, maybe only second to the *Shahi*. All the jinn here? Wealthy beyond measure."

Now it's starting to make sense. It's their own personal oasis – just like the sector of Lahore my family lives in.

Shamsa grabs a map from a stand near by, unfolding it. There are acres upon acres of shiny homes, stunning gardens, little festival centres, waterfalls and nurseries; everything you need to live comfortably and more. I bet any kid raised in this town will grow up successful. Yaqub should've weaselled his way in here.

Then I see the little note on the corner of the map: *Join us for only 100,000 jinn dinar a month!*

"There's a monthly subscription to live here?" I sputter. That's taking taxes to a whole new level.

"I think it's called rent." Shamsa shrugs. "So what's the plan? I don't see how anyone here will benefit from the Shamsa Fund."

All the skills I'd never use for myself are proving quite useful now. You might think to be a leader you need to know business, the ins and outs of a system – but I'd argue more than half the job is learning *people*. Their psychology, their wants, deepest desires, the fears and weaknesses they keep locked away.

"If you want people to follow you," I tell her, "it boils down to two simple choices: give them what they want or threaten to take something away."

CHAPTER 20

Noble Lies

I think back to the first friend I ever made.

Around four years old, I was the only kid left at the estate. Baba had business meetings at the office, and Mama had gone shopping earlier in the morning for new Eid outfits. Alishba had begged to go with her to the bazaar, while Ashar had snuck out to play soccer with his friends. The servants at the estate were more than equipped to keep me busy, but Baba saw this as a perfect opportunity to make new alliances.

It came in the form of a knock on my door.

His name was Taha Mansur, and he was a pudgy little kid with smudged glasses and a finger always up his nose. The son of an aristocrat, he had no problem making his way into the Rafiq estate for our "play date". Baba told me earlier that day that we needed to become fast friends. His father was a potential investor, and the more his kid wanted to come over to play with me, the better for our business. Or in the case of being four years old, more sweets for dessert.

Taha brought his collection of action figures – twice the number I had. He had all the superheroes, the special editions, the once-in-every-five-years collectibles. I wasn't particularly fond of muscular plastic men with goofy costumes, but I had to pretend to be.

When Taha Mansur sped to the bathroom after our brunch, I took his prized merman action figure and undid the screws; the next time Taha picked it up, it fell apart like a dry leaf. His tears were enough to fill the backyard swimming pool, but it was all part of the plan. Because not only had I taken something of his away, I was now offering it myself. I pulled out my identical merman action figure and gifted it to him as a token of our new friendship.

He loved me.

You might argue it was foul to break his toy, but I gave him the exact same one anyway. For him, nothing of value changed. But I gained a new follower.

Shamsa will have to do the same.

Baba would be proud to hear me now. "You've done the first part: offer money to those in need. But rich people can buy whatever they want with a snap of their finger. If you want to get their attention, you have to threaten something they already have."

She gulps. "What are we threatening?"

"The existence of this perfect town," I state simply. "All we need to do is poke and prod until we find something we can exaggerate into a larger issue. And that's when you swoop in, persuading them to vote in your favour if they want the issue fixed."

Shamsa frowns. "Sometimes I think *you're* more fit to be a jinn than I am."

I smirk. "There's a difference?"

Half an hour ago, Shamsa was a star. Now she's back under a shadowy cloak and creeping around town. We sneak into buildings, checking for bad plumbing or a creaking foundation – something wrong, something crumbling. No luck. The buildings are so sturdy that no matter how many times Shamsa attempts to punch holes in the walls, it's futile.

I scan the beige bricks; they're eerily similar to the ones made by my family's company. The only thing missing is the signature *R* at the centre of them.

Next we try the parks, examining the playgrounds for safety hazards. Everything's oiled and babyproof. Shamsa suggests we head to the Botanical Gardens, to find something potentially poisonous to point out. But

I can't do it. Not yet. Not when I don't know what Mama will say, do or think. My stomach stirs at the thought.

That's how we wind up at the centre square, a small welcoming festival in bloom. Slow carnival rides that elicit squealing laughter, swimmers dancing in the river that cuts through it, and booths upon booths of games and food lining the sparkling streets.

A couple enjoying skewered lizards chatter next to us. "I'm so glad that we play polo with Golnaz at the weekends. Who would've known she'd invite us to this exclusive neighbourhood?"

The wife nods furiously. "She's put so much effort into creating places where we feel safe. There are so many slum rats spoiling the capital these days."

My heart jumps out of my chest. I turn to them. "Golnaz invited you here?"

The husband eyes me warily. "She didn't just invite us. She built it."

I turn to Shamsa, and her face mirrors how I feel: punched. It all makes sense when I stop to think about it. Golnaz's multiple construction projects. This must've been one of them. She's been playing the long game, pulling in votes before this heir competition even began.

"She's in a different league now, isn't she?" Shamsa coughs out a laugh, gaze vacant as she eyes a string of paper fish decorating the outside of various shops. "I used to make those paper fish with her," she says. "They're a good luck charm. Meant to guide sailors safely to shore."

"Do you miss it? Hanging out with your siblings?" I know I do. Sometimes I think it's absurd there was a time when an invisible leader board didn't hang over our heads.

But Shamsa lets me know I'm not alone, as she gazes at the toy *Shahi* ships. "I would do anything to relive the days Golnaz and I skipped around the solarium, picking flowers and braiding them into each other's hair. I miss the easy laughter and the warmth." Shamsa smiles, and it's the saddest I've ever seen her. "Every summer, we'd play until dawn."

"Who says you can't any more?"

I never planned on it. I'd never pat the head of a jinn and grab their wrist, tugging them towards the festivities. But I do now, in the heat of the moment, in the hope that delight bubbles onto her face instead of misery. Shamsa isn't my friend, to be clear. She's a partner on my mission. And if she's not strong enough to complete it, we'll be stuck in the loser trenches together. So don't call me kind, or compassionate, or tender-hearted.

I see a crack in our operation and I'm filling it.

"Show me how to play this."

It's some kind of fish-catching game, and each player is given a magical rod that either attracts the fish in the tub or completely scares them away. Shamsa's unexpectedly great at it, as if she's somehow able to tug the water closer to her and lead the creatures her way. All I end up with is a stinky rod and no fish, and Shamsa's giggle skips through the air. Losing doesn't seem so bad after that.

We take turns throwing darts at moving targets. Then it's a quick break to the toffee apple shop. She decorates mine while I decorate hers. I'm plenty generous, covering it in things I personally find delicious: chocolate syrup, almonds, powdered sugar. She gives me one covered in raisins and cheese.

"You think you're so funny," I groan.

"That's a traditional jinn combination," she pleads. I could've believed her if she wasn't struggling so hard to hold back laughter.

We clamber onto a ride. It's a spinning chai cup, run on jinn flames that make my bum almost burn at the touch. It's for toddlers, and we do get a few odd looks, but there's no way I'm stepping onto one of their rollercoaster boat rides.

Compared to the start of the afternoon, Shamsa is beaming. All thanks to me. My heart swells a little at the thought. Until there's nothing more that we can enjoy, and only the path towards the Botanical Gardens stands in front of us.

My feet don't budge. It's as if the ground is quicksand, and I'm sinking, heart plunging to the floor.

Shamsa takes the first step. Smiling as she turns her head, she holds out a hand for me.

Like a boy drowning, I take it.

We walk silently on the path for a few moments, appreciating the bright flowers that line it. I can't even comment on how they smell *spicy* because the world is turning upside down, and my pulse is drumming.

It's Shamsa who pulls me out of everything, squeezing my hand.

"You asked me plenty of questions," she says. "Now it's my turn."

I swallow. I already feel my walls building up block by block, the windows slamming closed, shutters pulled down. When I don't respond, she knocks on the door anyway.

"Why are you afraid of the water?"

My pulse spikes. "I'm not."

"First was the train. And then you looked like you

wanted to puke when we saw the sign for boat rides into here. You act like it's poison."

"Not poison. An abyss."

She leans closer, and I have to suppress the urge to curl into a ball. The gourami is in my head again, staring, pulling me under. "Why?" she asks.

It takes a deep breath. A glance at the orchid sky. The lock in my heart shuddering as I poke a shaky key through. I don't know why my lips open and spill out words I've never spoken to anyone, relaying a nightmare that's played in my head like a broken record. It's my most vivid memory. My most hated. My most loved.

It might have been the golden light in the air, the soft hush of our voices, or the gentle caress of the flowers as they guided our path. Or it might have been that the eyes of the girl beside me, genuine and careful, held no judgement.

When I finish, she doesn't laugh. She doesn't tease me. She wraps my hand in hers tighter, sending me warmth. "Is it strange that I like you better now?"

"Because you can take advantage of my weakness?"

She laughs. "Because you're not as perfect as you seem. Perfection is boring anyway."

Before I can refute, bright orange flowers catch

my eye. The kind that crinkle at the edges, sunny and beaming. *Irises.*

My fingers reach over to pick them. I remember what Mama said they symbolize. Shamsa peeks over my shoulder as I collect a handful and weave the stems together. "Hold on," I grumble.

"I want to see!"

"Here." I plop the iris crown on her head. She doesn't get to see it, but with the way a smile cracks onto her face, she sure *feels* it. "You can always make new memories."

Shamsa giggles. "You're right. Ready to make yours?"

The path is ending, and a giant greenhouse shines before us.

I take a deep breath and nod. "Let's go."

CHAPTER 21

Runaway

I smell it first. Like the rush of a waterfall, a storm of scents attacks my nose. *Spice.* Sharp, stinging and overwhelming.

Giant flowers curl across the walls, towering towards the glass ceiling. Several ponds are scattered throughout, fish and frogs and mini ecosystems forging homes between them. As we step inside, the flowers turn towards us, as if they have eyes. Some even say hello, spurting pungent pollen in our faces. I hack out a cough.

It's incredible.

It's a world within a world. If I'm impressed, I can only imagine how much awe Mama would feel in a place like this. She could spend days here, or months. Maybe even a year.

There are human workers here, plenty of them, but their faces are shielded by translucent visors that shimmer at every angle. I'll have to sneak up close to get a better look.

Right as we enter, their heads snap our way. "Welcome to the Botanical Gardens," they greet in unison, smiles stretched to their maximum.

I nod while Shamsa waves to match their enthusiasm. Words don't form in my mouth, not when there're more butterflies in my stomach than there are in this garden. My limbs airy, mind wandering, it's Shamsa who keeps me moving forward.

We sneakily check every human on the trail. They're more than happy to chat up the princess while I glance through their visors, most likely thinking it'll buy their way out of here. The Botanical Gardens might be a gorgeous display of vegetation, but I notice the visors have a breathing filter attached. One of the workers confirms my suspicions.

"Some of the plants are poisonous to humans," he explains. "It won't do any damage to you on a one-time visit, but since we're working here day and night, it grows toxic."

He says it's no problem, but I still catch him and a few others coughing into their fists.

My gut clenches. *Where are you, Mama?*

We keep moving forward. Even as every face that's

not hers chips a piece of my heart away. Even as every step I take becomes slower, my body refusing to do what my mind is asking of it.

There, in the distance, a dark-haired woman is crouched around a patch of plumerias, caressing their petals. My heart leaps. I've seen this image before. So many times. Mama out in the courtyard, sitting with the flowers like they're sharing a joke, laughing as they kiss her cheeks.

The word tumbles out of me. "Mama?"

The dark-haired woman stands. Turns around to face me.

It's not her.

I collapse on the spot. Breath ripped out of me, exhaustion finally catching up, and the realization that it's never going to be her.

There are no more places to look – no more places to find her. I've crossed dimensions in search of her. Where else could she be?

It feels like one big prank. Like this is just some elaborate scheme Dadi cooked up so that I'd never bring up Mama again.

But then I think of the worst.

"Amir?" Shamsa's voice is quiet, like the crumple of a petal. "I'm sorry—"

"Shamsa, what if she doesn't want to be found?"

Her eyes widen. "What?"

I raise my head to meet her gaze, heart on fire. "What if she *did* run away? Even as far as the jinn realm. Because she didn't want anyone to search for her. B—because she doesn't like me."

Shamsa grips my shoulders. "Stop. That's not true."

"How do you know?" My voice shatters.

Shamsa's brow tilts upward, eyes reflecting a glassy apology. "She'd never hate you. There's nothing about you to hate."

I bite my lip. Her gaze is the only thing keeping me standing, holding me on course like a lighthouse to a lost boat. I want to believe her, but Shamsa always sees the light in things, always thinks the best of people. I've grown up only seeing the worst, knowing what hides under the mask. Perhaps all this time, Mama was wearing one too. Was she really happy in the estate? Did she want to leave the entire time?

Shamsa insists. "She loved you, didn't she?"

Did she? I have to ask myself. The more time passes, the harder that question is to answer.

But then I remember the hazy early mornings as she'd brush her fingers through my messy hair. The way she'd read me stories at night, have me hanging off every word. When she told me I'm her favourite person to go on walks with, because I let her ramble about all the different kinds of flowers.

"And sometimes, it's in the promises you make with each other."

That's how she described love. But I don't remember making any promises to her, or her to me. What is a promise? How deep can it truly be?

"Tell me about the promise you made," I say to Shamsa, sniffling. "Tell me everything."

We sit on a bench now, sunset glittering over a nearby lake, flowers bristling in the night air.

Shamsa kicks her feet up, hugging her legs. Her eyes stay focused on a star in the distance. "Remember when I told you about Golnaz cutting ties with me? That was a year ago, and after our awful conversation, I just wanted to roam the kingdom without anyone knowing who I was. Free, with no bodyguards, and no crowds that could corner me. I just wanted to see the lives of my subjects. See the magic that Golnaz refused to. So I transformed into a cat and snuck out of the *Shahi*." She releases a shuddering breath, and the water in the lake ripples.

"It was exhilarating at first. I hopped from one rooftop to the next, stole bites of street food, eavesdropped on random conversations. But the further I ventured, the more new places I saw ... which meant the less I knew how to get around. At some point, I ended up at the harbour. Next thing I knew, I was on a boat and it was *moving*. It was too late to jump back to shore. By nightfall, I wound up on another island off the coast of the kingdom."

I don't doubt Shamsa craving adventure, nor the way she somehow ended up in a place she shouldn't be. Sounds typical.

"There was so much forest. Then the sounds of drilling and machinery and metallic clanging. And heat ... so much heat. I couldn't stand it. I knew I'd strayed too far from home. I decided to reveal myself, force the boat back home, but I didn't have my royal ring on me. With thirty-two other royal children, not everyone knows our faces. I couldn't convince them. In fact, I did the opposite. The people managing the island thought I was a worker trying to escape. They—" Shamsa's voice tremors. "They started hunting me down."

My pulse gallops. I know how she must've felt – completely out of her element, chased by angry men who wanted to trap her. I glance over, and she's curled into herself, eyes shut like she wants to stamp down the memory. For a moment I think to apologize, call off the request to hear this story, but she continues like the words are a river hurtling down a mountain.

"I thought I was a goner for sure. From what I could tell, anyone who tried to escape that site wouldn't just be brought back. They'd be punished. I was so afraid, Amir. And no one wanted to help me. No one *could*. Everyone else was scared of protesting against the managers in charge. They had debts to pay. Families to feed. I was just some girl who was trying to escape the very destiny they were subjected to as well."

The lake goes still. "I hid. For as long as I could. But I heard rustling, and just when I thought they'd found me… It was a human. She told me the nearest route to the boat. Said that it was leaving in the next hour. That I needed to hurry. I followed her to the docks. But the hunters were close behind. When they saw she was helping me…" Shamsa clamps a hand over her mouth, muffling a cry.

"Hey, it's OK." I shake my head. "You don't have to tell—"

"They killed her."

My lungs collapse.

"We only got a few words in before it happened. She made me promise I'd change things. Something about how if she couldn't do it on her side, I had to do it on mine. I have to help the people stuck there, help everyone who's stuck in situations they shouldn't be in. That's why I want to be heir, Amir. Why I have to be."

When she turns to me, rather than resolve in her eyes, I see they're swimming with guilt.

CHAPTER 22

Back and Forth, To and Fro

Lights flash. The final challenge is about to begin.

Jinn point giant mirrors towards Shamsa as she strolls through the corridor leading into the council room of the *Shahi*. Apparently, the mirrors aren't mirrors at all – they're magical recording devices, and thousands of subjects of the kingdom will be watching. As if they're on the red carpet, each of the Kagra kids blows kisses or teases at their upcoming debate topics. One of the reporters shoves a mirror at Shamsa, and she yelps in surprise.

"What's your game plan?" they ask.

Trailing a few steps behind her, I nod when she glances my way. "Speaking the truth," she answers, just like we rehearsed.

I've written a thesis, provided ten different supporting points, and also highlighted key arguments that shouldn't be missed. As long as Shamsa hits each marker, the debate should tip our way. She says she's studied, but I still catch the writing on her palms, going so far as the inside of her sleeves. Past these bronze double doors, the council is waiting. Shamsa should be ready, prepared and well-versed. But ever since we came back from the gardens a few days ago, her eyes aren't reflecting confidence. They just reflect sorrow – directed at me.

I don't want her pity. I'm Amir Rafiq, all right? Even if I still haven't found Mama, it's not like it's going to break me. It's not like ever since she's been gone, a part of my heart broke away and never grew back. It's not like for a moment, as brief as it was, I wanted to embrace the hope that she was there.

"You may enter."

This is the only thing I can control now.

Shamsa heads inside first, chin tilted high and shoulders squared like I told her. But it's goofy when she tries it – she looks at the ceiling with her stomach sticking out. I should've never suggested it.

I'm allowed to walk in after, but my place is restricted to the corner of the meeting room, an arm's-length away from the teapot just in case anyone needs a refill. Because that's who I am these days: a butler too clever for his job.

The meeting room is grand, like all the other rooms on this ship. High, arched ceilings, walls with intricate panelling, and a giant round table atop what must be the softest carpet I've ever had the honour to touch. The malik and malika sit on the fanciest of chairs, not unlike the flashiness of their thrones. The council members are also already seated – all ten snobs – while each of the ambitious royal children file into their seats. Out of the thirty-three, ten are here for this meeting. Which means Shamsa has nine other contenders she needs to compete with. A one out of ten chance. Which is a ten per cent probability. It's not zero … but it's not exactly a promising win.

"Welcome, royals," the council member with the longest beard begins, his eyebrows so thick you can't even see his eyes. I've studied him and know that his name is Jawal, he has a pet pufferfish, and has divorced nearly eight wives. "The malik and malika, as well as the council, have decided to open up the table to any determined child ready to make a difference. The Kagra Kingdom has upheld itself for millennia, but not without its great thinkers. Do you have what it takes to be one of them? Then show us tonight."

Firas shoots out of his seat first, leaning against the table, his broad shoulders taking up as much space as possible. He wants to establish himself as the lion right off the bat, intimidating the others. I would've thought it a good strategy, but anything that comes out of his mouth immediately cancels it out. "So the fish are running out, yeah? The seafood market has taken quite a big hit because of it. So here's my plan: we take fish from another lake and throw them into the one that's lacking."

Hakeem, seventh-born, looks like a viper and talks like one too. "Why do you think the fish are missing in the first place? You're not going to heal a wound by slapping on a bandage."

Firas shakes his head. "Heal a wound? Who said anything about a wound?"

Sorousha holds up a finger. "I was thinking of the same problem, actually. If the fish population is dwindling, that means there must be something wrong with the river system. But if we want to think about immediate ways to recover our losses, we can try breeding fish in closed containments. Supervised and observed."

The council members hum at this, glancing at one another, scribbling on their parchments. The other children try to hide their disgruntled expressions. This is the moment Shamsa needs to jump in. I clear my throat, hoping Shamsa gets my signal.

She stands, voice more confident than I've heard in weeks. "The fish situation is but a small problem. The real trouble we've been having is unemployment. More and more people find themselves in the Kagra Kingdom each year, but because of the lack of jobs, they have nowhere to go but the slums. There's sickness, poverty and strife. How can we call ourselves the caretakers of the kingdom if we can't care for those who are most vulnerable?"

Perfect. I have to suppress a smile. She's set up our campaign brilliantly. Even the council members are nodding their heads.

"That's why I've started the Shamsa Fund. It's a charity for all those stuck in the slums, and for underfunded institutions. Their lives deserve to be noticed, supported and saved."

I'd break into applause if it was allowed. Textbook answer. Rehearsed and delivered with just the right amount of oomph. Ever since the campaign, I've seen a shift in Shamsa – a newfound confidence after realizing that outside of the royal family, she *is* liked.

The council members look pleased. Even the malika tears her gaze away from her nails for a split second, giving Shamsa a once-over as if she's seeing her for the first time. A satisfied smile snakes its way onto Shamsa's face, but it doesn't last long; the next one to rise from their seat is Golnaz.

She commands the table with the quickness of lightning. "Are you sure you're saving them, or are you making sure they never escape poverty?"

Shamsa freezes. "What?"

"Charity is a surface-level solution. It only provides temporary relief to a larger and deeper problem. Giving away money is just making the people who are suffering depend on you like a child depends on their mother. You need to build a bridge instead of just sending ships. Give a jinn a fish, and you feed them for a day. Teach them to fish, and you feed them for a lifetime."

Shamsa grips the table. Seconds pass. She says nothing. But even *my* mouth hangs open. Normally, I would jump to defend what we built, but a part of me realizes Golnaz might be right. We haven't thought beyond the first stage of how to help people.

"That's why I've started many construction projects so that the underprivileged get a foot in the door. The casinos, amusement parks, newer residential areas... I'm improving the kingdom while also providing jobs."

She's smart, this smoky sister of Shamsa's. She must have planned this years in advance just to get ahead of the game, and it shows her ambition and cunning. I have to commend her – it's a good play.

Shamsa's lips part, but again she slams them shut. Then it dawns on me from the way she can't even glance at Golnaz: Shamsa is scared. Terrified. Golnaz is the one wall too high to jump over. Never mind a wall, she's like an unscalable mountain. What happens when it turns out your role model finds you despicable? You run and hide. That's what Shamsa's been doing – keeping out of her way. But if she wants to be heir, she needs to leap into the spotlight and make herself seen.

Someone else makes the parry. It's another young one, twenty-fourth-born Imraz, who can't be much older than Shamsa. He's not the best speaker – too squeaky for anyone to take seriously, but his point is a good one. "How do we know your projects are what the kingdom wants?"

Golnaz doesn't back down, her smoky hair billowing larger. "I've already performed multiple surveys asking the subjects in the capital. I've only built what they desired."

Now. *Now, Shamsa.* She sneaks a glance at the writing on her palm, but before she gets a chance to speak the next eager child is up in arms. "That's not fair. You planned all this years ago." He slams his fists against the table, sparks shooting out like fireworks.

Golnaz stays still as a sentinel. "I was working while you were slacking. Is that what you're trying to say?"

The accuser sits back down, grumbling to himself. Shamsa grabs the chance and leaps to her feet. "I – uh … well," she stammers. "What about all the overworked wildlife and disturbed labourers?"

A council member cocks their head. "What do you mean?"

Shamsa's sweating buckets. "I mean the overworked labourers and disturbed wildlife." She chuckles nervously. "I've visited one of your projects – the elite neighbourhood just outside of the capital. It may look neat and perfect, but there are workers hidden in the corners working day and night. Don't you think you push them too hard?"

Good. I want to pump my fist in the air. Shamsa says as much as I hoped, not backing down. Even her voice sounds more stable. We can turn the tides, I know it.

But Golnaz doesn't feel the heat. Instead, the air turns suffocating. Grey smoke rumbles across the ground, tendrils looming over Shamsa like ominous shadows. "If your research is not thorough, then pointing fingers at my neighbourhood is easy. The workers are helping to build an invaluable addition to this kingdom. They know this job is a worthy one and are happy to be a part of it. That's why I have so many up for the task. They're rotated frequently."

As quickly as the accusation came, Golnaz swept it under the rug. I can't fact-check her claims right now. All Shamsa can do is continue the onslaught and cage her on the defensive side.

Shamsa shakes off the smoke. "Can you explain why you have humans working in an environment toxic to them?"

The room falls silent. It's hook, line and sinker with this one. Even the malik sits upright at that, peering over his belly. The malika finally tears her gaze away from her glittering nails, head cocked curiously. Meanwhile, the council members look to Golnaz, expressions uneasy.

If the air felt thick before, now it's a blanket. My chest is a cage, heart pounding as it begs for breath. But Golnaz is a storm cloud, smoke pouring off her in dark waves. "The poisonous plants are not a problem with the visor I've given them. It's a breathing filter to remove any toxins. Like I said, they're treated well."

My lips twitch into a scowl. Golnaz is lying through her teeth. I remember the workers coughing. I don't think those visors work at all. But since her voice is unwavering and her gaze resolute, no one questions the validity of her claims.

The reporters eat it up, their mirrors flashing, everyone craning to get the best angle of Golnaz as her hair billows behind her. I can already see the headlines: "New Heir Confirmed Already?"

"Wait, what about my fish idea?" Firas pipes up.

Hakeem hisses, rolling his golden eyes. "No one's taking you seriously because the rest of us aren't idiots."

Firas darkens, muscles bulging as he hurls a fireball at Hakeem. Hakeem transforms into a viper and slips away, but then he's launching his own fiery breaths, lighting the table ablaze.

Two becomes four, and four becomes eight until almost all the royal children descend into a yelling competition instead of a debate. Imraz screams as he slides under the table, while Sorousha's butterfly wings sprinkle peppery flecks that combust on impact. Hakeem and Firas are now in a wrestling match, Hakeem's long body wrapping around a writhing Firas. I can't even laugh when a fireball slings my way, ducking just in time before it singes my hair off.

Golnaz watches the chaos calmly, a small smile carved onto her face.

"Enough!" the malik demands.

The council adjourns the meeting, sliding their notes into their robes before they burn among everything else. They leave each child with a pat on the back. Some get encouraging quips, while others, like Shamsa, earn a participation badge: a nod of acknowledgement and nothing more.

"We shall announce the top five royal children who will give their speech during the heir ceremony," the malik says. "In no particular order, here are the names. Golnaz, for your insight."

No one's surprised. Golnaz plucks a piece of lint off her shoulder.

"Hakeem, with his great counters. Firas and his unbending will."

Unbending will? That's certainly one way to describe him.

"Sorousha and her quiet but valuable interceptions..."

I swallow. There's only one spot left.

"And Shamsa, with her valiant effort."

Shamsa scampers up to me, but it's not like the day we won the flame archery competition, all smiles and giddy butterflies. She's fiddling with her earring as her shaky gaze meets mine. "How was I?"

Something's off. No, *wrong*. It's as if this debate was nothing more than a teaser, and Golnaz's true plan hasn't even bloomed yet. As though we're catching sight of the seeds to her scheme, but not what's about to blossom. Where is she getting the money for this? The resources for all her projects?

"Amir? I'm sorry... Did I mess something up?" Shamsa clutches her hair. "Ugh. I should've practised another hundred times in the mirror!"

I walk past her. "We'll talk later."

Maybe it's not Shamsa. Maybe it's never been about Shamsa's skills. Not when someone else is controlling every variable of the equation.

It's time to talk with Golnaz.

CHAPTER 23

All is Fair in Love and Rule

I didn't expect to be let in so easily.

When I approach the wing that Golnaz calls home, I am prepared to argue with her hundred minions, tongue sharpened to cut through them. Instead, they part like a wave split down the middle, allowing me to pass door after door. Finally, the last steel gate looms over me, but I find it's already cracked open – smoke billowing out in great clouds.

"Come in."

I follow the trail of smoke, my senses assaulted by the thick, cloyingly sweet smell. I feel like I've walked into a storm cloud, grey and heady, lightning crackling in the air. As I step further, a figure lies on a settee near the back, shisha pipe pressed to their lips. With a soft sigh, the tobacco smoke coils towards me like an outstretched hand, ready to choke.

"I was wondering when you'd come find me," Golnaz says, propping up on one elbow as she looks me up and down.

"You're cheating," I accuse. It comes out quiet, stuffy, dampened by the thick air.

"Cheating." She hums, inhaling more smoke. "That's an interesting way to pronounce *competing*."

"First you tried to knock me down with your flame arrow when Shamsa started to gain the upper hand. Then you bought out her poet. Now there's these construction projects, winning over the rich by giving them lavish things they don't need, and the poor by giving them dangerous, life-threatening work. You're a fraud."

At this, she laughs – a sound like thunder, so sudden and rupturing I almost stagger back. "Do you think the rulers who sit on their thrones got there because they played fair and square? No, it's because they were like you and me, Amir. *Clever.* They outsmarted the rest and snatched the chance when they could. Look at your own family, for example."

My family? "What do you know about—"

"You're a Rafiq. The youngest son of the current CEO of the Rafiq Bricks Company in Pakistan. You have two older siblings. A busy father. And a missing—"

"Stop it," I huff, my breaths shallow. How does she know this? All this time that I've pretended to be a servant plucked from the streets, she *knew*?

"Your family has been doing the same for a century. You hunt down other brick companies and sabotage their dealings to stay on top. And the labour you hire? No. *Hire* is a generous word. Looks to me more like indentured servitude." Golnaz blows another round of smoke into the air, and I feel like I'm suffocating, windpipe crushed as I plunge into an abyss. "So tell me, Amir. Who's the fraud?"

"It's not true." I don't know if it's not true. I don't really know anything about my baba's company. I was coddled, caged by luxury tea parties and charity galas – hating every second of it. The only business I knew was the process. Make the bricks. Pack them up. Ship them off. What about all of Baba's investors? Supporters? But then Yaqub's solemn smile flashes in my head. What about the workers? The protestors? There's too much I don't know … too much I let myself ignore.

"It's not just *your* truth. It's the truth of this world. You need to step on others to climb to the top and keep them beaten down so they can never rise again. All I've done is the same. With her head stuck in the clouds, do you really think Shamsa is fit to be heir? You should join me, Amir."

I don't want to get involved in their politics. This kingdom is as foreign to me as Alaska. The question was never about who *I* thought was fit to rule. It was about doing a favour to get one in return. I'm helping Shamsa so she helps me find my mother. "I'm not interested. One thing I know is that at least Shamsa is honest with me. You keep secrets."

"Me?" Golnaz muses, her tone tinged with a terrifying amusement. "Are you certain Shamsa is as noble as she's led you to believe? I know the deal you struck with her. About finding your mother. But poor boy. It's *her* that's keeping the biggest secret of them all."

My pulse gallops. If she knows this much, could what she is saying be true? "What are you talking about?"

"Pitiful human. Run back to my sister if you want. But when you do, check what she wears around her neck like a medal."

I don't wait. My lungs already faltering, mind light-headed, throat clenched, I sprint out her rooms in a daze, stumbling towards Shamsa's room.

She's sleeping when I find her.

Leaning against the bay window, cushion at her back, lips parted slightly – it's like she sits in a painting, time eternal, the world quiet, stars twinkling. It's such a pretty night. Shame I'll have to step into the painting and ruin it.

"Shamsa," I announce my presence. She doesn't stir, not like the last time – when it was my room she slept in. Her blue hair glints in the moonlight, like strands of sea, falling over her shoulders in waves. I tug on one slightly. All I get in return is a soft grumble.

I don't have time for this. What's her secret? Is there one or was Golnaz pulling my leg again? I can't trust a single one of these jinn.

"Check what she wears around her neck like a medal."

Shamsa has always worn high-collared suits, gold jewellery layered thickly on top. But in her nightgown, I can see the barest hint of a silver chain that disappears down the silk. I reach forward, but my fingers coil back. What am I doing? It's just a plain necklace. Golnaz is playing with my head.

But then Shamsa shifts in her seat, and the chain pulls back slightly – revealing its pendant. An aquamarine, teardrop-shaped pendant.

I scramble back, knocking over a chair and hitting the side of her bed frame. The sound startles her awake. She lifts off her seat slowly. Every second that passes, that I see my mother's pendant around her neck, is another needle driven deeper into my heart.

"Amir?" She rubs the sleep from her eyes.

I can't breathe. When she steps forward, I step back. The movement is enough for her to raise a brow, finally noting the deep rise and fall of my chest.

"Are you OK?"

I point to the necklace. "Why do you have that?"

Her hand flies to her throat, clutching the chain. She swallows hard. "How—"

"Why do you have my mama's necklace?" It comes out like a growl.

Her eyes grow wider, breath hitched.

"You promised me no more lies."

"Amir—"

"All this time," I grunt, clutching my head. "All this time you paraded me around like a fool when you knew about my mother. I thought—" When my voice cracks, I bite back the venom. "I thought we were friends."

Shamsa nods, hair flying around her. "Of course we are. I can explain. Please, sit down."

I'm not stupid. I'd rip the necklace from her throat

myself, but I want this image of her betrayal seared in my brain, unforgettable. What's wrong with the world? What's wrong with *me*? Every time I open up to someone I find myself hoping, thinking there's a possibility that this world isn't entirely rotten. That it's not all transactions, debts and profit. I wanted to believe. I really did. And maybe that does make me stupid.

"I should never have helped you." The words escape before I can even think them, a gut reaction to this horrid epiphany. I step towards her, brow furrowed, voice coated in spikes. When she flinches, I don't feel sorry. "You don't deserve to be heir."

Her glassy eyes shatter.

I lurch closer like a looming shadow. "I never believed it. And I know *you* don't either. I'm aware you jinn are tricksters, but there's no trick that could've worked your miracle."

She trembles. "Y–you don't mean that."

"What are your talents? Skills? Smarts? I did all the work for you. Are you really able to sit on that throne without an ounce of shame, knowing that a pitiful human like me was the one you stepped on to get there?"

Tears stream down Shamsa's cheeks, glistening like the pendant around her throat. "I… I'm…" She can't even get the words out. It's pathetic. I don't care for her flimsy apology or claims of ignorance. I did everything I could for her, and this is how I'm repaid.

"What makes a good heir then? What makes a good ruler?" she asks, uncertain. Her voice is small, but her eyes glint with sorrow and anger, simmering with a challenge.

It strikes me like a slap. A good heir. A good ruler. What does that look like? What does that mean? "I don't know. I don't care any more," I choke. "Where's my mother?"

Her head drops low. "Amir…"

"Where. Is. She."

I give her ten seconds. I stand in front of the jinn princess I once thought to be my friend and wait. I give her one last chance.

And she fails.

I turn and walk out of her room and her life for ever.

CHAPTER 24

The Forgotten Shadows

I should go back to the human realm.

Smoulder my memories here like paper in fire. All I want right now is to burrow under my covers and take a long, long nap – so that when I wake up, I can convince myself none of this was real.

That the sharp pain in my chest is nothing but a dream.

It's like I've been steamrolled, every limb shaking with rage and hurt. But I can't go back. If I've already descended into this devilish realm, then I have no plans on leaving without Mama.

This time, I'll do anything. Chase any and every lead. Follow her heartbeat. Hunt down hints. Months or years, the time doesn't matter. She was the only one in my life who never lied to me. And now I realize how rare that is.

I'm out of the servants' quarter in an hour. Given how often the other servants have seen me leave with Shamsa, they don't question my exit. No bags, no belongings, there's only one thing I make sure not to forget: the slip of paper Yaqub left me.

It's another one of Golnaz's construction projects. Another place she's employed humans. And it's the best lead I have.

The address is a wonky recipe of letters. I doubt a map is going to help me. My best bet is word of mouth. I chase down a few lingering night servants and ask them about it, linking it to Golnaz's projects. Within ten minutes, I'm saved from making any voyages on my own. Golnaz is still recruiting, and she's more than happy to let new servants join. I can hop on a cargo ship by Fisherman's Bay and be there tomorrow.

Except it's a boat.

Just when I'm about to abort the mission, one of the other jinn servants leaps in, telling me about the camels — camels so tall they can hobble through the sea. I quickly tally up which is worse. A boat, where I'm close to water, can feel it mist on my cheek and taste its spice on my tongue? Or on the back of a giant camel, where the water is far below me, and I can squeeze my eyes shut and pretend I'm on a merry-go-round?

I'm going with the camel.

As I head down the *Shahi*, chatter scratches at my ears. The royal children are back in the tearoom, gossiping. I even find Shamsa's hunched shoulders over a steaming cup, letting it go cold as she eyes the floor vacantly. It's only when Firas claps her on the shoulder that she jerks alive.

"You really thought you had it, didn't you? Pretended to be all big and mighty. Who were you trying to fool?" Firas goads.

The other children laugh, pointing fingers. Shamsa folds into herself.

Hakeem's snake tongue flicks out with a hiss. "Shamsa, just be happy that we let you play in the big leagues. Especially since you can't run and cry to Golnaz any more about how everything's so unfair."

Another round of laughter erupts around the room like fireworks. Shamsa's eyes reflect glass.

I look away. I don't have any more time and energy to waste on betrayers. I won't spend another second thinking about how broken Shamsa looks, and how the bullying is only going to get worse now that I'm gone.

Someone else delivers the final blow. "Reality is different from fantasy, Shamsa."

I don't feel sorry. Not even the twist in my gut or the sandpaper in my throat will lead me to believe that. I speed up my pace, escaping the *Shahi*, darting between buildings, sliding past crowds, and lurching from shadow to shadow. By the time the moon hangs high in the sky, I stand at the border of the pink sea, sandy shore wrapping around my feet. The island I saw before – the one across the harbour – stands in the distance, heavy with spiralling trees and rising coils of smoke.

I trudge over to the nearby camel stables. They're giant, standing ten metres tall. With legs this long, these camels are bound to get me to that mysterious island in no time, right?

The camels are not a better idea.

If you were afraid of heights instead of water, this would be your worst nightmare. The camel hobbles across the sea at a snail's pace, swinging me back and forth.

Slow and steady wins the race, right?

Seated on its back with ten other jinn and humans, I am uncomfortable – but also feel strangely safe. I doze in and out, rocked by the camel's steps, until the whine of metal rings beside me.

The train of camels halts at a surprisingly large dock. It hosts the cargo boats I was supposed to hitch a ride on, plus a bunch of other stationed machinery ready to be used. And yet, it's quiet. Eerily quiet. The docks are mostly empty besides a few humans unloading cargo, but I have a feeling I haven't even chipped away an inch of what's to be found here.

We're led down a path into the giant forest, a cocktail of different flowers, weeds and plants. My neck almost snaps as I try to glimpse the tops of the trees. Their trunks twist and curl, soaring into the air like dark, ominous towers. I hear voices in the distance, echoes bouncing between the leaves. A single slimy river guides our path deeper into the forest.

The further we traverse, the more my stomach turns at the sight. The forest paths are ravaged, logs toppled, grass yellowing and patchy. Weathered, abandoned huts decay under moss and fungi. Tattered cloth litters the ground. It almost seems as if the shacks were fled in haste. Did a storm sweep through here?

I have the urge to ask where this wreckage is coming from, but I *hear* it first. A mechanical whirring, a low rumble that shakes the ground beneath us. Mixed with a high-pitched buzz that curdles inside my ears.

We pass a jumble of trees into open, razed space. Bulldozers trample across. Tree fellers slice through bunches at a time. Excavators grumble as they plunge into the dirt. I cough. Dust swirls in the air, so thick I can barely see the shadows that pass through it, only the haunting lights of the machines. But as a breeze sweeps by and the air clears, my stomach plummets. There's no way.

It's a brick kiln.

Chimneys being built, block after block, tower into the sky. The lake is being dug up, divided into squares. Some bricks are already lined up, clay moulded and prepared for shipment. Humans are working in organized lines, carrying piles upon their backs. My stomach drops. Both adults and children hunch over the clay, dirt caked on their skin, cuts on their hands, mindlessly toiling away. It's so late at night too. Where are the safety measures? Why are children working?

"Amir?"

I turn. Over the clanks of hammers and buzzing machines, his voice is a bell – calling me back to reality. I usually hate his grating tone, but now the familiarity is like a cup of chai, and I need to sip all its relief.

"Yaqub." I dart towards him, then take in his haggard appearance. "Are you OK?"

Yaqub looks duller since the last time I saw him. His collarbones protrude below his shirt, and his cheeks are hollow, thin skin stretched like an elastic band.

"Working hard," he huffs. "As always. I was moved to the excavation division a few days ago. It's been a lot of digging."

"What's going on? This looks horrible."

Yaqub shakes his head. "Bhaiya. I'm used to this. Is it that much of a shock to your pampered eyes?"

A sputtering breath escapes me. "How did something like this end up in the jinn realm?"

Yaqub holds a finger in the air, scoffing. "There's the million-dollar question. What if I told you we aren't in the jinn realm?"

I gape. "Could this be…"

"Just when I thought I was escaping that damn brick kiln I used to work for, here I am again."

My stomach lurches. "What do you mean?"

"We're at a border between both realms. And this brick kiln? It's the infamous Rafiq's."

He could've kicked me in the guts, insulted my mother, thrown me in a ditch, and I still wouldn't be as shocked as I am right now. I want to refute his claims, slap the accusations back in his face, but I can't.

Because the R-logo stamped into every brick at this kiln undoubtedly belongs to the Rafiq Bricks Company.

But *how*?

"This forest has acted as the border between the two realms for centuries. But now it's being destroyed to expand a human brick kiln."

Wait. *This* is the forest Baba talked about? The one that enclosed our kiln and limited our options? Rumoured to be haunted, notorious for disappearances— warned to hold shadowy creatures within. The forest that for so long kept our business on a narrow slice of land. It wasn't until a certain investor granted the rights to demolish the trees and expand our kiln...

My eyes light up.

"Golnaz!" I exclaim. "Golnaz is the investor who's tearing down the land."

Yaqub nods. "That's not all. You see all the pollution that's plagued this water? It's waste from the capital. Waste directly produced by Golnaz's recent developments in the city. The amusement parks. The lounges. The luxury. She's doing it all to sway voters in her direction. And the expansion of the brick kiln is helping to hide her evidence. We're cleaning up her mess."

"What?" It sounds ridiculous to me at first, but I can't deny what stares back. Bulldozers and excavators scoop up decaying trees and polluted water. Handfuls of rubbish are replaced with brick mounds.

Yaqub releases a bitter scoff. "She's planning to destroy this whole forest for her own gain and then pin the misfortune on the brick kiln."

"No..." Profits had increased. Stocks were skyrocketing. The company was seeing numbers that it never imagined before. But at cost of *this*?

My throat is dry like the air around us, words thin and wavering. "That can't be true."

I stand at this border, machines whirring, fires blazing, heart wrenched out of me.

All I see are children with vacant eyes, carrying more than they should. Men at the brink of exhaustion, one huff away from fainting. These are our workers. The people holding up the foundation of our company. And they're living like *this*, like zombies with no thoughts of their own.

Baba makes millions. Our family lives in a giant estate. We have farmhouses, a ranch with horses, and more luxury than we know what to do with. I'm the one who sits on a pedestal, acting high and mighty about what matters and what doesn't. I'm educated, and yet ignorant. Wilfully ignorant. I study with the best tutors in the country, go to the best schools, and *still* ... still

I ignore the cries of those who can't afford what I can.

What was I doing?

What I thought was merely a line between people like me and people like Yaqub is really an enormous fortified wall. I stand in the clouds, and he stands here – in the dirt. But now that I've fallen so low, I realize every snide idea I had of them was directly influenced by people like me. By people in power.

I glance down at my hands. They're filthy. I'm filthy.

All this time, I looked down on others for not working hard enough. I really believed that anyone could earn their way to the position I'm in. But there's always going to be someone rich that'll buy their way to the top.

What's hard work going to do for you then?

Commotion breaks out in front of us. A bulldozer is ploughing towards a diamond-shaped stone lodged in the ground, jinn and humans screaming for it to stop. They stand around the stone like a barrier, unflinching. I don't understand. Isn't it just a plain rock?

We join them, the stragglers who still live in the forest. They've come alive for this one act of devotion.

"What is this?" I ask Yaqub.

"It's a tombstone." Yaqub glances at me, almost hesitant. His chest rises with a deep breath. "They told me about it. Around a year ago, a bunch of humans began scoping this area. That's when a woman crossed the border and fell into our realm."

A human woman crossing into the realm of jinn? The hairs on the back of my neck prickle. There have got to be many.

"But then Golnaz struck. Brought her bulldozers and excavators and threatened everything… Nobody could do anything to protect the forest. But one of the first people who came to this island's defence was the human woman. She protested against Golnaz, but the princess wouldn't back down. Backed by all the resources and power of the kingdom, what did she have to fear? She bulldozed away."

Yaqub said many words, but the most important ones he tries to relay through his gaze. And I don't want to receive them. Not if it means what I'm thinking.

"The real horror happened when Golnaz's goons were hunting down a deserter. It was the human woman who helped her escape. But fate didn't have the same plans for the woman. She died trying to protect them."

A familiar name engraved on the stone stares back at me. A name that's been ringing in my head for the past year.

It's my mother's tombstone.

CHAPTER 25

Everything Changes, Only Change is Eternal

The sunset was beautiful that day. The last day I saw her.

We'd just finished dinner, bellies full and hearts warm, the post-supper laziness trickling into us all by way of the summer heat. I could've taken a nap, read by the window, or sat in comfortable, listless silence – but Mama took one look at the sky and rushed towards me, pointing at the coils of pinks, oranges and purples.

"Let's go for a walk."

It was just me and her, hands intertwined, even though I felt too old for it. But Mama had a way of making anything feel new, feel possible. As we strolled through the garden, lilies and petunias curling around our feet, the air simmered with magic. She found a spot at the centre of the garden, rich earth begging for a new friend. Mama reached for a sapling tree she'd bought earlier, her eyes glimmering as she turned to me.

"Let's plant it."

We spent the hour under the sunset on our hands and knees, dirt caked under our nails, making sure our new tree was snug and cosy. I was tasked with giving it a name, but the suggestions bubbling in my head didn't feel good enough. This moment was special, precious. *"Next time,"* Mama proposed, *"we'll think of a name together."*

Her words, soft as petals brushing against skin, caught the attention of all. The bees stopped buzzing. The crickets quietened. Even the sun dipped lower and shone its glorious rays over us like a spotlight.

"I didn't know what I was getting into," she told me. *"I love him, you know that right? And I love you too. That's what this business was supposed to be about. Love. We build bricks. The very foundation of loving homes, shelters that protect, walls that keep us warm. Yet this business has become the opposite of that."*

I nodded, even though I wasn't quite sure what she meant. But I heard love and ran with it.

"This isn't what I stand for. I can't just ignore this twist in my gut." She turned to face the sun, its fire lighting in her eyes. *"Changes will have to be made."*

I liked the way it sounded. So I echoed her. *"Changes will have to be made."*

The next morning, Mama was gone.

I remember that moment now, as I run from the place she died. When she first went missing, and I kept repeating the last thing she'd said to me, I truly believed the *change* she'd meant was her absence, that she couldn't handle the family business any more. That her only option was to run. But now I know.

My mother wasn't a runner. She was a fighter.

"Are you lost, boy?" one worker asks me. I ran off when the realization of whose tombstone stood before me trickled in. I couldn't look at it. Couldn't stand on the same ground she was buried beneath.

It's a jinn. They blend in well with the humans – steeped in the dark of night, you can't tell much difference. There's one expression uniting everyone, though: exhaustion.

"Don't get too close to the machines. Come with me." His voice is scratchy, as if he hasn't spoken a word in years. He takes me down a winding path in the kiln. We pass by other workers mixing clay, transporting the moulds or stacking bricks. "Stay close," he says. "If they catch you slacking, you won't get just an earful." He shovels a patch of dirt, readying it for the next pile of bricks to rest here, as casual as if he didn't just imply something horrible.

I stand next to him, shaken by his kindness. Despite what he just spoke of, the kinds of punishments the workers must receive here, he carries on. The twist in my gut only pulls tighter. *What if he knew I was the son of the owner? The potential heir to this business?*

I grab a shovel and try my best to mimic his actions. We're levelling the ground. It might seem simple, but my arms begin to shake only five minutes in. He's been working *all day*. "What do you do this for?" I grunt through another strike. What is he protecting? What was Mama protecting by helping them? I have to know. Why did she sacrifice herself for these people instead of returning to *me*?

The jinn man smiles for the first time since I've met him. He pulls at the chain on his neck, a lighter attached to it like a pendant. A lighter just like Shamsa's – one with the ability to record moments in time. He flicks it open, and within the small flame, I watch his favourite memory.

He's sitting under a shade of trees, wife and children chatting alongside him. They're munching away on leaf sandwiches, and one of his sons burps so loudly they all erupt into laughter, afternoon sun glowing behind them. But then the image shakes, as if the ground began rumbling. The trees behind them fall, keeling over like toppled buildings. His family scatters in a flash, like a flock of disturbed birds. The flames of the lighter dissipate, memory ended.

"The expansion of this kiln means they've already demolished half of the forest. And I don't think they'll stop here," he says, eyes glimmering as he strikes the shovel again.

My lungs seize. "Why haven't you tried to stop this? Fought against these working conditions?"

"We have," he scoffs. "Organized protests. Stood our ground. Sat here for hours to block their developments. But when they bring the heavy machinery, what can we do? We can't compete against their power. If you can't beat them, join them. We need the money to eat and provide for our families."

"But this isn't right—"

"That's not for us to decide." He grunts. "The rich and powerful are the ones who create these corrupt situations in the first place. Then they find the poorest and most desperate of us to do their dirty work. You're complaining to *us*? About the way we bring food to the table? Don't make me laugh."

My throat tightens. "What changes would make it better?"

"Liveable wages, proper safety equipment, no more contracts that we can't get out of. The human woman who came to us a year ago spoke of those changes. That when she left, she would do everything in her power to see them through. But Golnaz got to her first. She ordered the patrol against her."

I force myself to swallow the bile that rises up my throat. The truth is this: Mama cared. She wasn't a background player in the company, or rather, she didn't let anyone force her into the margins. Before Mama and Baba met, Mama had worked as a receptionist and known many businesspeople, seen them come and go, listened to their insider exchanges – but Baba struck her as different. He didn't talk of riches and fortune; he was still the heir to the company and giddy with the potential it possessed. Mama saw in him a man who could focus on the right things – on ways the business could provide for *others*. She believed it could happen.

And when she realized Baba wouldn't help her, she set out to do it herself.

I think of the last time with Nani, when she asked me a question that burned deeper than the kiln fires.

"Don't you feel it, Amir – that invisible weight? Have you ever thought that your hands hold on to something more than your own future?"

Back then, I stared at my stubby fingers and saw nothing. But when I look at my hands now – I can *feel* it. The ability others weren't born with. The power of being raised as a wealthy man's son.

When you're me, hard work doesn't matter. Things don't need to be earned. I have the special skill of making the decisions instead of having to choose between them. That's what Mama wanted me to understand. That's the reason she married Baba, to make changes that can only happen at the top.

Baba led me to believe that being an heir was to shake enemy hands and strap on fake smiles. That it was about how much money we could vacuum into our pockets, and that any other goal besides that didn't matter. And I started to think the same way. I looked at Shamsa, called her innocent and naive, when she only held a belief that was pure and hopeful. One that came from Mama. I'm the one with the twisted senses.

Mama died protecting the girl I just abandoned.

"Amir!" Yaqub sprints up to me, chest heaving. "Why'd you run off?"

I can't keep it from him any more. "This is my baba's brick kiln."

He rolls his eyes. "I know I started the rich-boy jokes, but you don't have to take it this far."

"And that tombstone? It's my mother's."

"Wait – what?"

My heart is already torn open; it was only a matter of time before it spilled out. "You were right Yaqub. I'm a rich kid. I didn't come to this realm to earn money like you. I came in search of my missing mother. And now I've discovered why she never came back. She couldn't."

Yaqub's jaw hangs. His eyes flicker between me and the rest of the kiln, a mixture of hurt and anger flashing within them. I know he must be furious with me – the son of his employer, a boy who has so much more than him. I don't expect him to pity me. And I definitely don't expect him to grab my shoulder and ask me the same question I've been trying so hard to push down.

"You have to do something, Amir," he pleads, the words so fragile it might break if he speaks louder. "What will you do?"

I jam the shovel into the dirt, exasperated with myself. Everything I've done so far was a step in the wrong direction. I can't stand on the sidelines any more and let people tell me what to do.

People said Shamsa was a loser for not having fire powers.

People said I should step into a mindless life I didn't ask for.

People said my mother ran away.

I don't care what they have to say any more.

The image of a blue-haired, beaming girl pops into my head. And how I left her behind. Stuck in a room full of her taunting siblings, doubling down as they crushed her dreams. Called her words a fairy tale, her ideas childish. The very things that will make her a better ruler than them.

I pull at my hair. I left her there, with her heart torn and bleeding. All because of a misunderstanding. Mama gave her that pendant, the one so special to her, not because Shamsa wanted it. But because she deserved it. Mama saw something in Shamsa I've been too stupid to realize.

For all the horrors Golnaz has subjected others to, there's one truth of hers that rings in my head at this moment. *"Charity is a surface-level solution."*

She was right. Charity may soothe the after-effects, but it doesn't prevent the cause. Generosity isn't what's going to really help the poor. Changing the system is.

"Changes will have to be made." I echo Mama's last hope. "If I choose to inherit this company, then it's not going to look like this."

Yaqub straightens, hope simmering in his voice. "How?"

A clang rings through my bones. The jinn man from earlier strikes his shovel again, but this time his chain gets caught on the wood and the necklace breaks apart, lighter thudding against the ground.

My eyes widen.

"Hold on a moment. Can I see that one more time?" I ask him.

He picks it up and hands it to me, brow raised. "All right."

I flick it open, and the memory plays again. The burp. The laughter, and then the shaking. I peer closer. The trees are falling. But when I notice who stands in the back, my hunch proves right. There, in the corner of the memory, is Golnaz. Clipboard in hand, directing bulldozers as they trample the forest.

My lips break into a smile.

"Amir?" Yaqub questions.

I dangle the lighter in front of him. "The people here don't have a voice. No influence or power or strength to change things. But the people at the top *do*."

Yaqub hums, as sceptical as I was when I first understood. "So we're going to climb the tallest mountain?"

"We're going to crash the heir ceremony tomorrow."

And save the one girl who believed in me even when I didn't believe in myself.

CHAPTER 26

Finders Keepers

The capital is buzzing.

Crowds have gathered near the *Shahi*, its pink flag flapping in the afternoon breeze. It's giant, immortal, almost castle-like in the way it has merged with the land. Moss grows on its hull and vines snake up the sails. There are vast gardens on different levels, and I can see the council members running back and forth on the promenade. The stage at the front is so high it overlooks the entire island, and the current speaker capturing everyone's attention is seventh-born Hakeem, forked tongue hissing out lies.

"No one knows what they actually want," he bellows into the magic microphone, voice echoing across the island. "But I do."

"Says the guy who's never taken public transport, never made his own meal, and wouldn't know the price of a gulab if it stared him in the face," Yaqub mutters. We're on a carriage heading towards the ship. Beside the stage, there's seating for the five royal children who prepared their own speeches – the cream of the crop. I look for Shamsa's electric-blue hair. But I don't find it.

Yaqub seems to notice too. "You don't think she dropped out, do you?"

I curse under my breath. This is my fault. I'm the one who told her she had no skills of her own, when none of my plans would've worked without Shamsa's innate brightness. "We'll find her."

"Look at the predicted votes." Yaqub points at the skinny waterfalls behind the ship, each one reflecting an image of a different sibling. A number shines below them, and I have to suppress a groan. Golnaz is ahead by a strong portion.

Even though I disapprove, I'm not surprised. The voting for heir is public, but ballots are only held at the capital, where Golnaz has strategically poured her resources. Stealing funds and extracting fortunes from the other islands, she's remodelled the kingdom exactly where it matters: for the rich jinn in the capital.

Gambling houses that leak money, amusement parks with distractions at every corner, lavish stores with fabrics and items imported from all over the jinn realm.

What's not to love? For the capital citizens, Golnaz is an angel blessing them with luxury after luxury.

But then I catch a dark rope hanging at the top corner of the stage. Except it swings back and forth against the breeze. It's not rope. It's Shamsa's furry cat tail. "There!"

She's up before the second blink, slinking from the corner, heading down behind the stage. If we lose her, I can't imagine how many thousands of cat-shaped crevices we'll have to check.

I keep my gaze glued to her as we slide off the carriage near the hull of the ship. Her ears disappear behind some plumbing. This ship has hundreds of entrances, from actual doors to mouseholes in the wood.

"Trust me," Yaqub promises as I stare sceptically. "I had a short but eventful time as a cleaner on this ship. I know where the dungeons are *and* the secret passageways."

He scrapes away some of the moss on the hull while I keep lookout, watching for any guards that might question why two kids are harvesting vegetation off the *Shahi*. Yaqub snickers when the moss falls away and a hole big enough for our bodies is exposed. He clambers inside, and without another option, I pinch my nose against the decaying smell and step in behind him.

It's dark, empty and damp. We splash through shallow, ankle-deep water. Machines whir in the distance. Footsteps resonate above us. The commotion of the crowds fades into a hush.

"This way." He leads, quiet voice echoing within the vast hull. We leap over pipes, past abandoned barrels, and shimmy over rotten planks. This ship is ancient, so old I can almost smell the centuries of blood, sweat and tears soaked in its wooden boards.

We slip into a long dreary corridor, nothing but hollow walls with bars running down the length of it. Whispers and grunts echo from the shadows.

"Shamsa?" I call hesitantly.

But instead of a streak of electric-blue hair, I see smoky curls billowing into the air. Golnaz.

Yaqub and I swerve around a corner, peering round the wall. Golnaz is hovering next to what seems like a few of the ship's engineers. They talk in hushed, urgent voices.

"The carnival rides and aqua shows are using too much water," one engineer explains. "All the water we collect from the surrounding waterfalls and sea passes through this ship. The more we use, the more it decays. And right now, we've used more than we should have in such a short period of time. It's decaying faster than we can repair it."

Golnaz's haunting voice rises above the others like a storm cloud. "I need the rides and entertainment running. At least for as long as the voting lasts. Once I'm heir, shut them down."

"But—"

"I need to deliver my speech," Golnaz cuts them off, drifting away like a breeze.

Yaqub clicks his tongue. "We need to show the kingdom her true colours before the ceremony is over."

"How long do we have?" I grunt, thinking of what the realm would look like if Golnaz took control. But Shamsa keeps popping into my head instead. Shamsa, and the chance she never got.

"Not sure," Yaqub says. "We need to move quickly."

Another flick of a tail in the darkness. I know she's here. "Shamsa?"

The ship creaks impossibly quieter. She can hear me, but she won't come out.

I dissolve into a jumble of everything I've never said, even if it looks like I'm talking to air. "I'm sorry. About everything. For mistrusting you, leaving you during the most important moment, not realizing you're everything this kingdom needs."

Her breath hitches. "I am?"

"And more. You're a better friend than I deserved to have."

"That's not true. I'm a terrible friend. I lied to you. I don't deserve your kindness, let alone the kingdom's."

All the confidence Shamsa gained through this competition has shattered like glass, and I'm stepping on the shards all around us. I try to pick one off the ground. "I know why you lied. Why you had to."

A pair of red eyes glint in the darkness. "Amir…"

"And I know you don't believe in yourself. That's why you didn't think you could win on your own. Why you still don't. Why you feel like you're only running for heir to fulfil a promise out of guilt." My hands clamp into fists at my side. "But you don't understand, Shamsa! My mother didn't make that promise because you owed her. She made it because she *believed* in you."

Shamsa the cat lurches out of the shadows. With a blink, she's back in jinn form, brows tilted and lips trembling. "Why would she believe I can change anything? All I spout is nonsense about destiny, fairy tales and childish dreams."

"Fairy tales are only as unreal as the power to make them true. It's not that dreams can't be achieved, it's just that some people never get the power to make them real. Who told me that? You, Shamsa. And you're right.

All these grown-ups and the people pretending to be them tell us that kindness is useless. They say being generous is childish. That hoping for something better is nothing more than foolish dreams. I say we stop listening to those voices. If they don't want to use their power to make fairy tales come true, then I'm going to help someone who does."

Tears well in her red eyes. She leaps forward, arms wrapping around me in an embrace. "I'm sorry too. For keeping your mother's death a secret. I never should have made you search, made you wait. I wanted to tell you. There were so many moments I thought I would explode because of keeping it from you. But you were part of the promise, Amir. When your mother died saving me, she told me to save *you*."

My heart lodges in my throat. "What?"

"She told me, '*My youngest son… I'm worried about him the most. Will you find him and tell him that he can choose what life he wants to lead, what kind of man he wants to be? That even if he makes bad decisions, falls and stumbles, everything will still be OK? That he won't be loved any less for failing?*'"

I feel like a fool. I've lived my entire life in fear of mistakes, of angering the wrong people, of making *bad decisions*. Mama's last wish was to tell me not to.

"'A life you choose for yourself is better than one chosen for you.' That's the last thing she told me."

A long breath rattles out of my throat. I may have been born into this life — the life of a spoiled brat — but I can change that. Even if it means failing and stumbling along the way. Even if it means fighting against the very people who put me here in the first place.

Shamsa fidgets with her collar. "Why'd you come back?"

The realization only hits stronger after what she's told me now. "Because I realized I don't just have the power to take. I have the power to *give*. And you were trying to tell me that from the beginning."

A wry smile melts onto her face. "I don't blame you for not believing in me. It hurts. When you realize your hero isn't who you thought they were. But so many people are like that — rulers, businessmen — it makes me wonder if everyone who touches power is like that. It makes me wonder if *I* would turn into that."

"I'm not sure you have the smarts for that."

She punches my arm — and smiles.

Yaqub clears his throat. "How about we discuss the plan before the heir ceremony ends and none of this becomes worth it?"

"Right." I glance between Shamsa and Yaqub. "Yaqub and I talked about it beforehand. Our main objective is to make sure Golnaz doesn't win the vote. There's two parts to this plan. First, to sneak you on stage so that you can give your own speech and talk about the injustices plaguing the other islands. And while you're giving your speech, we display the evidence."

Shamsa stares. "How?"

"We have a memory lighter that proves Golnaz is the mastermind behind everything. She's even been expanding my father's brick kiln into jinn territory. But we need a place to show it. Somewhere the entire capital will be able to witness it."

"Easy," Shamsa chirps. "The ship's flag. Burn it with the lighter's flame and it'll blaze with the memory."

"That would require us to make it to the top of the ship," Yaqub exclaims. "That's, like … numerous floors of security."

I drum my fingers against the wall. "That won't be a problem for me."

Yaqub scoffs. "And what are you going to do?"

"What every rich boy does best," I reply. "Be a brat."

CHAPTER 27

Worth Falling For

There's one thing nobody gets right about rich people: we don't have a *certain* look. The only way you can tell us apart from a commoner is by the way we carry ourselves.

That's what I tell myself when I scavenge for a crisp kurta and wash the mud off my body in a nearby bathroom. Even though I'm not wearing my armour of designer shirts and a gold wristwatch, it doesn't mean I'm not a Rafiq. I was raised to command. I slick down my hair, squeeze the creases out of my clothes, and push my shoulders back. When I look in the mirror, I find a spoiled rich boy staring back.

Perfect.

Yaqub has gone to prepare Shamsa for the ceremony, guiding her through the ship, keeping her safe and out of sight until the moment that matters. I, on the other hand, need to clamber up ten floors to burn the flag of this ship.

I rush up the first flight of stairs. The floorboards groan like an old echo. When I reach the next floor, it's guarded by burly jinn in black kurtas, shades sitting on their noses. I have to pass through the gate to get to the next set of stairs. All I need to do is convince them to let me through.

I strut towards them, chin high and expression bored. My eyes scan the room like I own the place, and I brush my fingers along the walls and cabinets as if inspecting them. One guard's gaze finally snaps up, and that's part one of my plan complete. Let them notice *you*.

"Can I help you?" he asks.

I maintain my aloof expression, releasing a hum of contemplation. "I'm not sure about this place."

His lips twist into a confused scowl, fang hanging over his chin. "Excuse me?"

I force a flicker of exasperation in my eyes. "Are you not aware of why I'm here? I'm the investor from the human realm. You are the ones who called *me*."

He flinches, trying to hide the worry swimming in his gaze. His fingers flip through scheduling books, but now's the time I need to enact step two: take control.

I don't let him finish sifting through. "I've already toured the hull. Now I'm here to check the reports. I can't invest without seeing the projected numbers. Where can I find them?"

"R–right this way … sir." He eyes me up and down, no doubt wondering what a twelve-year-old human has to gain from this heir ceremony. But control comes in a pair with confusion. You create enough confusion, and everything is in your pocket.

He leads me past the gate and up the next several floors, unlocking the codes. When the door opens, the smell is what hits me first. Pulpy parchment and the dry, musky scent of trees. There must be thousands of documents lining the shelves of this room, and none of them are organized.

"Thank you, I'll look through myself," I tell him. He nods quickly, happy not having to spend another second talking to a spoiled human.

I don't really care about this kingdom's ledgers; what I did accomplish was sneaking my way up the ship with no suspicions. Glancing out of the window, a garden full of greenery waves to me. It's a solarium, with everything from palm trees to crown imperials growing in the corners. Despite it being sunny outside, grey smoke curls around the plants. I peer through the glass and find the X on my map: the pink flag flapping against a lavender sky.

This could be the short cut I need. The solarium looks ancient, with rotting panels, dense moss and a thick carpet of grass, but I'll have to risk its crumbling steps.

Pushing the solarium door open, a gust of smoke hits me. It's dense, crawling across my skin, looming above like a storm cloud. The plants shiver as the smoke curls around them, caressing their leaves like a soft kiss. I fan the fumes away, following the glimpse of purple sky that shines through it.

But there's something else amid the smoke. A figure stands at the balcony of the solarium, overlooking the kingdom, shisha pipe pressed to their lips. With a soft sigh, the tobacco smoke coils towards me like an outstretched hand, ready to wring my neck.

"There you are," Golnaz says, leaning an elbow against the railing as she looks me up and down.

My pulse gallops. "Pleasure to see you again," I lie through my teeth. I ball my hands into fists to keep myself from screaming. This is the jinn who killed Mama and so many more. That looks at vulnerability and sees an opportunity to climb higher. I would do anything to have her disappear for ever. I would do anything to have her bring back Mama.

It takes everything in me to keep my voice level. "I know what you're doing. And I'm going to expose you."

Golnaz cocks her head. "And what is that, little boy?"

"You steal resources to fund nothing but luxury entertainment in the capital. You raze the forest of another island to expand my father's brick kiln. All so you can gather enough riches to pull the votes in your favour."

But she counters with scathing words. "Do you really think Shamsa is fit to be heir? You should support me, Amir. Who's going to blame your company for destroying that island when it no longer exists? I'm expanding your kiln, while you're helping to silence the protestors. Our interests are mutual. When you become the owner of the business, your company will be booming thanks to my help. We'll have a partnership that transcends realms. We'll be untouchable."

Her confidence doesn't come from nowhere. The arrogant sharpness in her voice stems from the fact that all she's saying is true. If I let her continue to demolish the forest into dust, the brick kiln could grow three, four, five times bigger. Our fortunes would overflow like the sea during monsoon season.

The Amir from before wouldn't have cared. He'd see peddling, toiling workers and think they were victims of their own bad decisions. That poverty had been their choice. But the Amir I am today knows that's not true. And that the voice they so desperately need is only available to someone else.

I know who I think would speak their concerns aloud. "Why did you betray Shamsa?"

"*Betray* implies that I was on her side in the first place." Golnaz laughs airily, like wind rushing past my ears. "Back in the day, we got along like all children do – I, her admirable baji, and she, my naive little sister. But she stayed that way even as we grew. She clung to her fairy tales and talks of destiny like a last lifeline. It became worse when we found out she was a disgrace: a jinn with no fire powers. I guess she needed to live in a fantasy to cope with it all."

The time I mocked her for not having fire powers barrels back into my mind. Shamsa's pout. Her defeated slump.

"If she'd stayed quiet, I wouldn't have minded her. But instead, she visited the people – reduced herself low enough to converse with ordinary citizens. She once brought a beggar to the *Shahi*, pleading with our father to find him work on board. Her head was in the clouds.

Every day it was *'Baji do this, do that!'*. She spoke of dreams like they were possible. She never understood that reality doesn't work that way."

"It could. If the people in power wanted it to," I state, shaking my head. "You knew that. You knew Shamsa had a way of making others believe. And you were intimidated by that."

"Intimidated?" Golnaz scoffs. "No one would ever want such a childish ruler."

"Childish, or hopeful?"

Golnaz cocks her head, smoky hair swirling faster. "You sound quite confident for someone who doesn't have evidence. Unless, that is, you do."

I step back on instinct. A dead giveaway. Her dark, hollow eyes creep over me like a horde of insects, prickling the hair on my arms.

"What are you hiding?" Her voice surrounds me, echoing, slithering, as if it drifts through the smoke in the room.

I need to get to the flag. Shamsa should be ready by now. She could take the stage at any second. I dart away, flailing to clear the smoke. But it's stronger now, thick and suffocating. I can't see a metre in front of me. Shoving my hand in my pocket, I check for the lighter. My heart drops. It's gone.

"Looking for this?" Golnaz laughs from behind me, a trail of smoke curling around her hands. When it evaporates, my pulse stops. The lighter glints between her pointy fingers.

"Give it back—"

She throws it over the balcony.

I chase it, sprinting over to watch it hurtle down the ten floors of the ship and plop into the pink sea below. Our only evidence. The key to the plan. And now it's gone, sinking further to the bottom of the ocean as the seconds tick by.

Golnaz hums. "I knew there was never a chance Shamsa would win. And now you do too."

No.

She does have a chance. I would bet my entire fortune on it. It's *me*, I've been the one clinging to old traditions. Dismissing her claims because I was ignorant enough to think being heir meant being a figurehead, a robot for shaking hands and giving false smiles.

I don't think I'll do it. Even at the last second, as I sprint towards the balcony and my foot leaps across the ledge, I think this might be the day I die. Some might call me a fool. Some might say this isn't worth it. But I know it is. Mama died for this very reason. And it just so happens I might too. Like mother, like son.

My breath hitches, my heart stops, my body evaporates. For a second that's all I feel – nothing and everything simultaneously. I see the crashing waves below me, and, in them, Baba's face. I hear the rumble of the water, and in the background, my laughter mingled with my siblings'. I feel the sea vapour tickle my skin, just like Mama's caresses as she read me to sleep.

When the water takes me, I imagine it's her arms.

CHAPTER 28

The Promise that Sparkles Between

Water crushes me – front, back, above and below.

I see the glint of the lighter as it sinks slowly, like snow drifting in the air. My fingers reach out, scrabbling for the metal until it's in my hands. Finally. But even though I grasp it, I can't move. I'm an anchor thrown into the sea. Deadweight. All I feel is an abyss sucking me in, breath by breath, pulse slowing like a broken engine.

"Amir."

My heart throbs. It's Mama's voice.

"I've been waiting for you."

I should be scared. I should be sceptical. I should wonder when this strange dream of jinn and magic will come to a close. But her voice – Mama's voice that I haven't heard in a year – is like the toll of a bell, holding me still, freezing the beat of my heart. There's nothing more I want than to chase it, run into her embrace, feel the warmth of her arms again. This is it. Mama's here. And she's been waiting for me to open the door.

And I see one in front of me – outlined in gold, bright against the dark abyss of the ocean. I knock on the door. "Mama?"

The door creaks open, and light pours over me like the waves of a golden ocean. A memory greets me – the clover field at our farmhouse, air sweeter than honey, summer sun spreading her rays over us like a blanket. I see Mama settled on a chair in the colourful garden, flowers swirling up the frame to kiss her shoulders. I'm breathless, my laughter ribboned with joy, happy about something that doesn't matter any more. But what did – Mama's bright smile as she saw me, arms open wide to catch me. She always caught me. And even now, as I'm falling, as the darkness ebbs into eternity, I can feel the warmth of her embrace.

"Amir!"

A flash of bright pink with blue stripes captures my vision. Gourami? It's swimming towards me, mouth opening and closing in a silent shout. Its dark eyes glimmer in the low light. There's a tug on my shirt. Pressure wrapped around my body. Then I'm hurtling through the waves until sunlight hits me across the face and I'm gasping for air.

"Amir, are you OK?"

Strands of blue brush against my cheek. Eyes fluttering open, I'm welcomed to the sight of Mama's pendant glittering back at me. I glance up, meeting a worried gaze. "Shamsa? What are you doing here? What about your speech—"

"I saw you falling into the sea! And I know how much you're afraid of it. Why would you do something so ridiculous?" Her voice edges into a yell.

I finally realize the reason my fingers are trembling is because of how hard I'm gripping what's between them. Unclasping them, I show her the lighter.

"Amir," she exhales, eyes glinting. "The speeches are over. We didn't make it in time."

I freeze. The cold of the water catches up to me, and not even Shamsa's hand on my shoulder can thaw the ice that coats every inch of my skin. "No…"

She bites her lip. "I guess dreams can't carry kingdoms."

"I just risked death to save that lighter. Tell me we have another chance," I sputter.

"Who's the one serious about this competition now?" Shamsa chuckles, but the sound is brittle, tinged with remorse. "I'm sorry."

A crackling groan pierces the air. I whip my head to the side. Is the *Shahi swaying*?

The crowds just below it scream and shout, sprinting away from it as if it's caught on fire. But I don't see any flames. What I do notice is parts of it crumbling like chalk against a blackboard, crashing down to the ground.

"Guys!" a voice to our left yells. It's Yaqub. His wide eyes ring the panic alarm inside me. "The ship's about to fall!"

"What?" Shamsa gasps. "It can't be."

The water roars louder. Rumbles ripple across the valley. The ship begins to tremble, shaking us all off our feet.

Yaqub wheezes. "All the water Golnaz is using for her attractions passes through the ship and it's too much for the *Shahi* to manage. It's about to collapse."

"Can't they shut them down?" I yell over the noise.

"It's too late."

If the ruckus was noisy before, now it's mind-blowing as the hull of the ship erupts, planks splintering like a firework, water rushing out like it's being pumped. The entire structure careers and whines. The solarium floods. The boardwalk crashes piece by piece. Crowds back away with a shriek, trying to escape down to the capital. But that's not going to cut it. There are dozens of waterfalls that intersect right where the *Shahi* acts as a wedge. If it collapses, it takes this entire island with it.

Shamsa knows it too. "No, please..." She looks back and forth, across both sides of the ship. The water is already spilling over the embankment, tugging jinn into its whirlpool. The entire city will drown.

But not before we do.

A tide crashes down on us, throwing Yaqub, Shamsa and me in different directions. I'm gasping for breath, head bobbing up and down, but the force is like an anchor tied to my feet, yanking me down no matter how much I flail.

"Amir!"

Shamsa reaches for me, the waves moving with her. With every thrust of her arm, it's as if the sea answers, swirling around my body. The ship groans again, planks shattering as water blasts out of it. A giant tide threatens to crash down. I want to shut my eyes to it all, but instead I focus on Mama's aquamarine pendant around Shamsa's neck, glinting in the sunset as the shadow of the tide looms over me.

Swallowing one last breath, I wait for it to crash down.

But it doesn't. The tide curls around me like a hand, cradling my body into the air. How? I glance around to see tidal waves in all directions held back, trembling, one giant wall of water that could crash at any second but somehow isn't. Then I see her. Shamsa rising to the sky on a tower of water, arms outstretched, shaking with the effort of her magic.

I can't believe it.

All this time, Shamsa cried over not being able to control flames. But it was because water was her element.

CHAPTER 29

Turning Tides

Screams chorus below us.

Jinn are running for their lives as the sea overflows and gushes onto the land like a bleeding wound. For most jinn, water is an extinguisher, soaking the vitality out of them. But Shamsa's no regular jinn.

Riding the waves like they're nothing more than stepping stones at her feet, Shamsa patters towards me, still in the clutches of her aqua fist. "I can … control water," she gasps.

I can barely get the words out myself. "Yes. You can. Your powers are just as weird as your personality."

Shamsa's face erupts into a smile. Like a staircase, the water curves and bends to form a set of descending platforms. Shamsa settles me down against a rock first, waves crashing below.

"I have to stop this," she says, looking to her own

hands as if she can't believe it herself. "I— I need to stop it."

She dives back in, arms spread, pulling upon the tides like the moon itself. A giant wave threatens to drown everyone in the capital but it halts mid-crash, as if suspended by strings. With a yell, Shamsa raises her arms and sends the waves backwards.

But it's not just any direction. She may look in a trance, eyes glowing and body floating, but she guides the tides around the kingdom, between the islands and back out to sea. The water that rushes through the streets is pulled back with her might, coughing jinn escaping its clutches.

Even when the ship collapses with a roar, she doesn't let it destroy the life beneath. Her waves swoop in, catching the slabs of metal and hurtled beams.

I could sit there and watch her for hours, mesmerized by the way she controls the water, but then I remember the metal lighter that sits in my palm and I push to my feet. I leap from plank to plank, stumbling across debris floating in the waves. I have to reach the ship's remains – a mountain of wood and metal and ancient magic. The flag is still fluttering in the wind, pink and bright and waiting to sing one final song.

With a grunt, I jump off the last plank and onto the hill of scraps, cuts tearing into my skin as I climb higher. Shamsa's still controlling the waves, pulling them back from the crowds, roping the water into streams that arch over the capital and into the sea. She's busy. It's my turn to step up and finish what we started.

A gasp escapes me. I slip down the edge as more wood crumbles. But I'm not going to stop now. I climb, the retreating sun daring me to climb as high as it. The flag is just out of reach. One more haul. One more grunt. And I'm there, heaving at the top, pink fabric whipping above me.

I flick the lighter open. Hold it as high as I can. The tiny flame catches on a thread and, within seconds, fire engulfs the giant flag, and the memory plays like a movie for everyone to watch.

The forest. A pleasant jinn family. Machines like monsters leaping out of the dark and razing the forest. Golnaz at its helm.

The jinn of the capital, drenched and heaving, watch with wide eyes and mouths gaping. Even as the memory ends, the flames continue burning, a single fire in the sky against all the water. Shamsa relaxes her arms, and the waves finally calm, a single moment of peace before the storm will undoubtedly strike again.

She jumps out of the water and back onto land, addressing the crowd that stares at her with halted breaths. Shamsa dips her head; unheard of for a princess. Her glittery red eyes are wet with tears.

"I'm sorry. To everyone. All the people of the islands who are pushed to the back and taken advantage of. For so long, the kingdom's coffers weren't used in the places money was needed most. It was recycled between the people who control it. But I don't stand for that," Shamsa declares. "I want to change it all."

Her words hang in the air, balancing on the edge of a tightrope. The crowd is quiet, almost frighteningly so. *Please,* I beg in my mind. *Can't they see she's the one?*

Then gradually, like dominoes, the crowd lower into a kneel, heads bowed. Their voices thread together, echoing across the valley.

"All hail Princess Shamsa, saviour of Kagra Kingdom!"

"Shamsa! Shamsa! Shamsa!" they chant. "To our new heir, Shamsa!"

Shamsa's eyes twinkle, gaze sweeping across the crowd like a caress. She shakes as if this was never possible, as if the most unexpected, unheard of, borderline sacrilegious turn of events has just occurred. She's so unsure of herself that even if the crowd carved out their hearts and handed them to her on a platter, she still wouldn't believe it. But you can't deny what's in front of you.

Her lips tremble, but she bites back the sob, choosing to stretch her mouth into a smile instead. A smile royal enough for a princess, but warm enough for a friend. And that's it. That's how I realize.

Smiles. Cheers. Fists in the air. Crying jinn embracing their saved loved ones. All of it possible because of Shamsa.

She places a hand on her heart, voice shaky but burning with joy. "Thank you … my subjects."

My chest thumps, heart growing three sizes bigger. Despite living my life at the top, always looking down on others, I feel my legs bend.

I'm kneeling. Not because she'll wear the crown or because she just saved my life. But because if there's anyone I'd follow, human or otherwise, it'd be her.

My jinn princess.

CHAPTER 30

The Will to Let Go

There's so much I want to tell you.

I have these dreams, of a young boy too shy to say anything. Most days, he keeps busy in his den of darkness and silence, confined by the cold of his own thoughts. And in the worst moments, he forgets who he is, who made him, and who he's supposed to be. But in those moments, he thinks of you, Mama. The beacon with gold in her eyes and birds in her voice. The one that burned brighter than the sun, gaze always holding a challenge.

It's you I clung to. And in turn, it's you who caged me.

I let the world be defined by you. I let every joy be destroyed if it meant being reminded of you. And every pain I felt was because of your loss. I let myself devolve into a shell of a boy, hope punished, dreams stolen and wonder erased.

If the world didn't want you, I didn't want it either.

But standing before the girl you saved, Mama, I think I've grown a little.

"We knew each other for less than a day," Shamsa whispers, her voice low and soft as we stand on the train platform. "She asked me what a princess like me was doing there. I told her I was lost too… All my siblings had big ambitions, and there I was, on that strange island, talking of destiny and adventures. But she told me…" Shamsa grins, cheeks tinting rosy. "She told me that was exactly what she liked about me."

My lips quirk upward. "Sounds like her."

"I told her to come with me. But your mother said she needed to go back. That she'd find her way out no matter what. When she handed me the necklace around her neck, she said, *'Promise you'll never lose your wonder or hope or dreams. Promise you'll run for heir, Shamsa. Because it's people like you I want at the top.'*"

My throat clenches, and a single tear runs down my cheek.

"Amir?" she says, hand on my shoulder. "I'm sorry."

I can't help the tears now. In all honesty, I'm afraid. I'm scared to face a world without you, Mama. Even when you went missing, when I couldn't see you or hear you any more, I moved through life with the belief that you were still here – somewhere, breathing the same air and looking to the same sky. But now that you're gone, now that I know you're completely, entirely gone, I'm terrified to see what remains and not find anything worthy at all.

"It's going to be terrible. Tough. Nothing we've ever faced before. And it's going to happen whether we like it or not," Shamsa says, squeezing my shoulder tight. "But you know what? We'll survive. It'll be dreadful, but it'll be all right."

Shamsa will face harder challenges as heir, more nasty people with sinister agendas. And I too will face a world without Mama, trying to move forward as grief weighs me down. There will always be tougher obstacles along the way. But we will survive. We must. We go on and find new things to hold on to that keep us living.

"Thank you for telling me. For teaching me. For everything."

She giggles, and I'm alive again, seeing something new. Something worthy. Ever since being declared heir, a beaded circlet has adorned Shamsa's head, but it's weaved with irises – from the same flower crown I gave her. I didn't expect her to keep it, let alone wear it proudly.

"And thank *you*. For calling me a great friend."

"*Good* friend actually. Don't get too cocky. What are you going to do without me now? I'm almost worried for the kingdom. The heir is going to lose her most trusted adviser."

Shamsa elbows my side. "The *Shahi* is going to be rebuilt, slowly but surely, and definitely stronger this time. But most of the coffers are going to be spent on the islands around the capital. I want to make sure schools are getting the funding, workers are being compensated, and outside communities see some life again."

I smile. The image of the future looks bright.

"And I'm going to try to talk to Golnaz," Shamsa whispers, like a secret, like something so fragile she's scared it'll skip away in the breeze. "Right now she's being held in the underground prison. I want to know if there's still a reason to be sisters again."

It's not going to be easy. Once a bond between two people is cut, it can never be regrown, only tied back together. But that cut doesn't disappear. "Do you think you can forgive her?"

She glances at me with a lopsided smile. "The odds aren't impossible."

A distant rumble echoes towards us. The train is approaching, wheels screeching as it slows into the station. I leap to my feet, brushing off my trousers.

"I've been meaning to give this to you." Shamsa inches closer and reaches around her neck. "Your mother's necklace. You should—"

I shake my head. "Keep it. My mother gave it to you for a reason. Just don't think of only her when you wear it. Maybe remember me a bit too."

Shamsa snorts, choking on laughter. I join her. It's a beautiful day. Too beautiful for a goodbye.

"I want you to remember too."

The train honks for people to board.

"What do you mean?" I ask.

Shamsa rummages around in her pocket, pulling out her memory lighter. "Keep it."

"What's on it—" I try to flick it open, but Shamsa clamps her hands over mine, cheeks flushed.

"Don't look yet," she tsks.

Warmth bubbles in my stomach, and a smile breaks onto my face. "Fine. Since it's the last time you get to order me around."

The train honks again. I clamber up the steps, waving to Shamsa as the wheels hiss into a roll again.

"Amir!" she calls out.

I poke my head out of the window. "Shamsa?"

"Make me a new promise" – she grins, smile wider than the summer sun – "that when you compete to rule your own little kingdom, you'll let me help you."

A scoff sputters past my lips, but I can't help mirroring her smile. Reaching out the window, I flick her forehead. "You're already acting cocky."

The wheels creak into a steady rhythm, honk blaring one last time. Shamsa laughing is the last thing I see before I settle into a seat by the window, pulling out the lighter. It has the same nicks and scratches as the one Shamsa had that held her memory with Golnaz. Did she want to give me a piece of her childhood? But when I flick the lighter open, a new memory is burned into the flames.

It's us in that plastic town, walking towards the greenhouse. Flowers are dancing in the breeze, bright and colourful. And there's me, braiding them together, reaching towards Shamsa to set the flower crown on her head. My heart gallops. She would've had to capture this memory before knowing Golnaz's true intentions. Before being given a reason to erase the old one.

I laugh, echoing our joy in the memory, and pull the lighter to my chest.

"I know you'll miss her, but at least you have me."

I whip around at the voice. A kid with a patchy scalp loops an arm around my shoulders, poking my cheek like we've been best buddies for centuries. I'm squeezed to the edge of the train seat.

"I'm giving you three seconds, Yaqub," I grunt. "You better get off me."

Yaqub doubles down. "What's rich boy going to do? We're still in the jinn realm."

I reach over and grind my knuckles against his head while he yelps, pinching my side.

I'll finally let you go, Mama.

Because there are things I need to grasp firmly now, things I need to pour all my wonder and hopes and dreams into.

Even if I didn't find you in this realm, I discovered something else.

The path I choose for myself.

CHAPTER 31

The World at the Top

"I need you children to behave, you hear me? *Behave*."

Dadi's in one of her moods again. Today is Baba's wedding, extravagant and busy and, of course, newsworthy.

The wedding has two purposes: offering our family a fresh start and serving as a distraction from all the negative press. When it comes to controversies, Dadi only has one mindset: shut it down. It's why we're all suited up and looking our best, so that the world will look at us and think, *How on earth could these sweethearts do anything bad?*

It's been a month since I came back to the human realm. Explaining where I went was a slight problem, but I brushed it off as extra courses at an overnight academy. Dadi liked the answer, so no one else bothered to investigate. But now, as Baba leads us through the white carpet runway on a vast ranch, cameras flashing and reporters sticking their microphones in his face, questions abound.

Baba waves, the vivid flower arches behind him helping paint the perfect picture of a gentleman. Dadi lingers in the back, hawk eyes keeping close watch. Ashar, Alishba and I are forced to stand in the corner, lips strained as we smile like this wedding is the best thing to happen to us. When kids are in the picture, Dadi said, reporters tend to play nicer.

"Congratulations on the marriage," one reporter says. "We've all been hoping you'd find peace and love again. But we understand there's been some rumours about low wages, missing workers, and harsh working conditions in the Rafiq brick kiln?"

Another journalist shoots to his feet. "Is it true that most of your labourers are in debt to the company? And that's why they can never switch to a different job?"

Baba smiles tightly. "Untrue. The financial situation of each worker is personal. Our employment has no strings attached."

Another journalist raises their hand. "What about the low wages? Compared to other brick companies, yours is one of the more frugal ones."

Baba laughs it off like someone told him a little joke. "Nonsense. If our wages are comparatively low, we make up for it with different bonuses."

It's back and forth like that — journalists on their feet with an onslaught of accusations, Baba as calm as an imam while he brushes them off, and the cameras flashing brightly, blinding my eyes.

"Have your kids been getting along with your new wife?"

I flinch at the question. It's inappropriate for the topic at hand, but when have press conferences been anything but a feeding frenzy? Baba looks at the runway carpet, then at Dadi, then at us kids. Alishba squeezes my shoulder.

"She's making an effort," he says, clearing his throat when the words come out crackled. "I've got three talented kids. Everything takes time."

The journalists turn to us, beady-eyed and bustling like meerkats. Suddenly, we're the main attractions — the future of the Rafiq Bricks Company. Microphones swarm our way.

"Can you please give us some insight on this? Do you kids agree with your father about the accusations against the company?"

Ashar beams his sunny smile, earning the hearts

of all. Slicked-back hair, pearly white teeth, he's the company's poster boy, perfect distraction from the real problems. "Of course. I think our father answered these defamatory accusations well. I'm going to study abroad in the coming months, so I hope to hone my skills and be as brilliant as him one day."

They eat it up like starving vultures, telling him to look this way and that for some extra pictures.

Alishba can't let Ashar steal all the thunder. She wrenches the microphone her way, lips in a tight smile. "I also think the accusations are uncalled for. These are all baseless rumours with no evidence. Our father is handling it gracefully."

And then they pivot to me, little Amir Rafiq's turn to answer the question. The last press conference Baba held was several years ago, when I looked like a loaf of bread – barely a boy. Not a single one of these journalists expects something from me, nor do they see any sort of concrete attachment to the company. I'm the youngest. The last in line. The easiest one to weasel their way out of all this.

But in the corner of my eye, I see a crowd of workers who've gathered at the press conference, eyes sunken and backs hunched. Their gazes drill holes into us, and their twisted scowls show just exactly how much they disapprove. I see Yaqub, hands clasped together, buzzed hair still patchy in places. Food is the usual thought flickering behind his eyes, but this time, all I see is a candle of pleading. I told him my plan, and how I'll need his help with it. To actually *make a difference*.

"The way the company is handling everything is terrible," I say into the microphone, eyes boring into the camera. "But that'll change when I'm in charge."

Acknowledgements

Second books are a bit like getting up on stage in front of thousands without knowing exactly what you want to say, but the audience is waiting expectantly, hanging off your every word, waiting for you to make or break it. When I wrote my debut, *Nura and the Immortal Palace*, there were no flashy stage lights and no audience. It was like any other rehearsal. But with this second book, I was plunged straight into the limelight, scrabbling for what I wanted to say. Thankfully, there were people at my side to tell me it was OK if I didn't know, and that all I had to do was be honest and tell a story true to me.

To my agent, Melanie, you're always patient with me, and for that I can't tell you enough how grateful I am. You listen carefully and truly try to understand my perspective on all things, and that's a skill I'm sure you've honed over years. I'm so glad to have you on my side.

To my editors, Ruqayyah Daud and Gráinne Clear, where do I begin with you two? You both saw me struggling to write a sequel, and, like saints, extended the grace to allow me to write whatever I wanted. Without you two, there's a high chance I'd still be writing this book, never feeling satisfied. Thank you for telling me it's OK to fail, but that I shouldn't keep wandering in the shadows of doubt, when there's a light at the end of the tunnel if I just look up.

And of course, I'm ever grateful to the teams supporting this book – the lovely Root Literary family, you're always making big moves. To the team at Little, Brown, thank you for giving this book another home. To my advocates at Walker Books, you've helped me achieve my author dreams and so much more, and I know I can always find a genuine corner of the publishing world with you all.

I've always felt extremely lucky when it comes to covers, and that's a blessing made by my brilliant cover designers Tracy Shaw and Maia Fjord. Your creativity and expertise are things I'd love to watch unfold in real time. And just when I thought I couldn't get covers better than my debut, Khadijah Khatib and Hazem Asif once again prove that magic does exist, because how is their talent real? You guys are visionaries.

To the people who stood by me when I was clouded in doubt, thank you. Ream Shukairy, Sara Hashem, Elizabeth Urso, Threa Almontaser, and Christina Li – publishing would be lonely without you all. Thank you to my parents, my sisters, and the relatives across the world who are always cheering me on.

And my deepest appreciation to you, my readers.

We'd love to hear what you thought of

#AmirandtheJinnPrincess
@WalkerBooksUk
@maeedakhan